THE ONE DAY OF THE YEAR

🏭 Angus&Robertson
An imprint of HarperCollins*Publishers*

*Note: Applications for permission to present
this play by professional and amateur
companies must be made to the author's agent
Hilary Linstead and Associates
P.O. Box 1536, Strawberry Hills, NSW 2012*

Angus&Robertson
An imprint of HarperCollins*Publishers,* Australia

First published in Australia by Angus & Robertson Publishers in 1962
Students' edition 1962
Reprinted in 1993
A & R Playtexts edition 1976
Reprinted in 1977, 1980, 1981, 1984, 1985, 1986, 1988 (twice),
1990, 1991, 1992 (twice), 1993, 1996, 1998 (twice), 1999, 2000, 2001
by HarperCollins*Publishers* Pty Limited
ABN 36 009 913 517
A member of the HarperCollins*Publishers* (Australia) Pty Limited Group
http://www.harpercollins.com.au

HarperCollins*Publishers*
25 Ryde Road, Pymble, Sydney, NSW 2073, Australia
31 View Road, Glenfield, Auckland 10, New Zealand
77-85 Fulham Palace Road, London W6 8JB, United Kingdom
Hazelton Lanes, 55 Avenue Road, Suite 2900, Toronto, Ontario M5R 3L2
and 1995 Markham Road, Scarborough, Ontario M1B 5M8, Canada
10 East 53rd Street, New York NY 10022, USA

National Library of Australia Cataloguing-in-Publication data:

Seymour, Alan.
The one day of the year.
(A & R playtexts)
First published Sydney: Angus & Robertson, 1962.
ISBN 0 207 13330 1.
I. Title. (Series).
A822'.3

Printed and bound in Australia by Griffin Press on 79gsm Bulky Paperback White

23 22 21 20   01 02 03 04

AUTHOR'S NOTE

ONE ANZAC DAY during the mid-50s I was walking through the back streets of the Sydney suburb of Summer Hill. It was afternoon, and the celebrations were well under way. In lanes and alleys near pubs I saw men lying in what used to be called a drunken stupor. Broken bottles abounded in the streets.

Now I happen to like alcohol; living in England, I deplore the fact that it is hard to get a really cold beer, and I enjoy discovering good French and Spanish wines. But the beery haze which had settled over the most solemn day in the Australian calendar seemed to me then somehow excessive and dangerous in that it tended to amplify the already heady sentimentality of that day. As long as men fuzzily exchanged rich, romantic memories with wartime colleagues, so long, it seemed to me, would any sensible analysis of the individual engagements of those wars, and indeed of war itself, be delayed. Why not a play about the essential hollowness of the Anzac Day maunderings?

Another theme came along and temporarily obsessed me, and until it was formed into a play and written out of my system the proposed Anzac Day drama could not come to light. One has to earn a living, and although I had managed to complete the first play around the edges of business hours, it was not until I gave up regular employment and began full time writing that I could get on with *The One Day of the Year*. In the meantime the theme had developed and the family in whom the central argument would rage was well and truly established in my mind.

But when I began work in earnest something unexpected happened. I found myself liking, almost loving, the older generation, represented in the play. Originally these had been, at least at a philosophical level, the villains of the piece. The sheer persistence of their long and scruffy, but somehow dignified battle to cope with the overwhelming facts of the life of this century (war—depression—war) forced me to respect them. The young man, Hughie, as the play progressed, had to come to this too: not to agree with them, but at least to find some compassion. This is the real theme of the play: Hughie, reacting against his family's lack of intellect, is eager for the rigours of intellectual truth and so must acquire some education of his emotions before he can be said to step towards maturity. It seemed to me only truthful to suggest that his father would suffer no radical change of heart and would end in ritualistic chanting as he had begun.

A play should be studied in the social, theatrical and even geographical context of its time. If the Australian drama of the 1950s seems to be excessively "naturalistic" (always a misleading term, for to make · things appear natural requires a high degree of conventionality and artifice) this is not because Australian playwrights write only "neo-realist" plays. It is because these have been the safest ones commercially for entrepreneurs to produce. Many dramatists have been experimenting on paper with verse, post-expressionism, Brechtian epic-style theatre complete with music and dance and doggerel, high rhetorical drama of neo-classical bent, and the Theatre of the Irrational. Now that prevailing trends abroad have shown again the diversity of the theatre's resources perhaps Australian theatregoers will see some native drama not wedded to neo-realism. I believe very deeply, though, that the neo-realist play, dated as its form may now seem to critics nourished (?) on Ionesco, Beckett and Pinter, does have a major strength very appropriate to a nation, like mid-century Australia, seeking to develop a theatre which represents the national image. Each country has its own habits of speech. If playwrights wish only to reproduce mechanically some of the well-known tricks of this speech (*vide* the "'Struth, stone-the-crows" school of earlier Australian plays and films) then neo-realism is indeed a dull and superficial method. But selectivity, compression and absolute accuracy to the *emotional* truth behind the speech can produce something quintessential which reveals far more than the way a nation speaks: it somehow catches, isolates, illumines the way its people think and feel. That a national emphasis in drama need not be unhealthy has already been proved by Australian writers: there is more criticism than flattery of Australia and Australians in most of the plays produced in recent years. Idiomatic writing, by the way, is not, as so many seem to think, confined to "naturalistic" drama. That great internationalist and anti-naturalist, Brecht himself, wrote in a highly special colloquial German devilish to translate.

The weaknesses of *The One Day of the Year* are all too apparent to its author and have already been critically discussed. To take a few examples . . . The girl, Jan, is the least convincingly written role. She began as a type and despite (or because of?) feverish and frequent rewriting has refused to emerge as the individual I had wanted her to be. The weakest scene, I think, is that of her intrusion in the third act, although the final rejection scene between Jan and Hughie runs it a close second. This is not because Australia is still a frontier society and its writers only good at describing mateship, as one disingenuous critic suggested, but because Jan started out badly and I just never got her right.

May I make a suggestion? You are to study, to analyse and, presumably, to criticize this play. Plays are written to be performed. If you can somehow *produce* it as part of your study you will really find out how good or how bad it is. To get down to the bedrock of a play nothing can equal

[5]

the repetition of rehearsal, the fusing of movement and feeling with the words, the ruthless examination, disintegration
and re-integration of the text which must take place in any
preparation for performance, even an intimate student one.
But performance can prove even more than an aid to
critical assessment. In bringing characters, literally, to life,
student actors will realize that plays are not primarily
about ideas or conflicts or controversies. The theatre's great
task and accomplishment is the study of humanity—a study
as urgently necessary now as it ever was in this uneasy world.

ALAN SEYMOUR

ACT ONE

The Cook family's house in one of Sydney's inner suburbs on the Western side of the city.

A multiple set, main areas being the kitchen; the "lounge"; and HUGHIE'S *study, which is a glassed-in sleepout at the side of the house. Each of these may be presented as fully or as sketchily as is thought fit. Furniture throughout is cheap, dowdy, bought long ago on T-P.*

The kitchen is the old enclosed-back-verandah type, with a table, chairs, gas stove, sink and primitive home-made kitchenette.

The lounge-room which should occupy central part of set contains an old lounge suite upholstered in brown Genoa velvet with flower patterns. Some of its springs have gone and in places it sags. An occasional table near lounge and an ashtray on a stand.

HUGHIE'S *verandah room has bright contemporary curtains along its "louvres". In the corner a small bed, next to it a little table with portable radio, piles of books, exercise books, notebooks. On clothes closet nearby stands a modern camera of superior quality and a few packets of films for it.*

DARKNESS. *Noise is heard, men's voices, talking. Even before the lights are up we can tell that one of them is*

[7]

drunk or at least on the way to it. Lights come up on kitchen. ALF *and* WACKA *are seated at table.* ALF *is in truculent mood,* WACKA *negatively acquiescent.*

ALF. I'm a bloody Australian and I'll always stand up for bloody Australia. That's what I felt like sayin' to him, bloody Pommy, you can't say anything to 'em, they still think they own the bloody earth, well, they don't own the bloody earth. The place is full of 'em. Isn't it? Wacka! Isn't it?

WACKA. Yes, Alf.

ALF. The place is full of 'em. Poms and I-ties. Bloody I-ties. Wherever y'look, New Au-bloody-stralians. Jabber, jabber, jabber. The country ain't what it used to be, is it? Is it?

WACKA. No, Alf.

ALF. 'E gets in the lift, 'e says "Seven". Like that. Not please, thank you or kiss me foot. Just "Seven". I get'm all day, jumped-up little clerks, think they're God Almighty, well, they're not God Almighty, I know'm, I take'm up and down all day, you think I'm not sick of that lift. Well, it won't be for that long, I'll show 'em, won't be that long now. You see when I get my new job. Did I tell you about my new job? I'll be right when I get my new job. None of this up and down, up and down all day. [*He drinks.*] 'E says "Seven". I says: "Wotcher say?" 'E looks me up and down as if I'm a lumpa dirt, his nose wrinkles up, he dunno he's doin' it but I seen it, I seen it so I says, more polite like, layin' it on only he don't see I'm havin' a go at him, I says Beg Yr pardon, sir, did you say Seven or Second? I wish I had a quid

[8]

for every time I've had to ask that in the last thirteen years. And he says, "I said Seven, old man." Gawd, when they start old man-n' me . . . Bloody Poms. I thought of a few things I could've said but there was a dame in the lift, she was eight months gone if she was a day. I thought what I'd say'd make you drop that colt right 'ere and it'd be me who'd have to deliver it, wouldn't be the first time neither. You dunno what it's like, shut up in that thing, it's like a bloody cage, being polite to every nohoper every day, all day, holdin' yr horses when they tread on yr foot or ask silly bloody questions or bloody near insult you in front of the mob, they give me the dries, they do, they give me the screamin'—[*by now almost beside himself*] I'm as good a man as them, who says I'm not? Who says I'm not?

[*The front door bangs.*

ALF [*continued*]. Who's that?

MUM [*from hall leading from lounge room*]. Me.

ALF. Frighten hell out of a man. [*To* WACKA] She bangs that door every time she goes through it, you wonder why I'm grey.

[MUM *has come through lounge unbuttoning overcoat.*

MUM [*coming into kitchen*]. Are you on it again? [*To* WACKA, *neither with nor without enthusiasm*] 'Ullo, Wacka.

ALF. You want one?

MUM. No, just had a cuppa tea at Mabel's.

ALF. Have one. Go on. [*He is pouring it.*]

MUM. I'm not havin' beer on toppa tea. It's too cold for beer anyway.

ALF. Never too cold for the old amber, love.

MUM [*glares at him*]. How much've you had?

[9]

ALF. Oh, get orf me back. [*He pushes glass towards her.*]

MUM. I don't want it.

WACKA. I'll 'ave it.

MUM. You've got one in front of you already.

WACKA. I know. [*He takes glass, drinks.*]

MUM. Hughie not home?

ALF. Had a late lecture.

MUM [*getting electric jug*]. I'm cold. Think I'll make meself a cuppa cocoa.

ALF. Cocoa! [*A long disgusted look at her, then*] I feel sick.

MUM. Gimme a look at you.

ALF. You put your jug on.

MUM. Gimme a look at your tongue.

ALF. I will NOT give you a look at my bloody tongue.

MUM. Don't you swear at me. Anyway, I don't need to look at your bloody tongue. I can see your bloodshot eyes.

ALF. Very funny. [*Turning his back on her*] Wacka, have another drink.

WACKA [*suddenly waking up*]. 'E's awright, Dot. 'E's bin good as gold.

MUM [*at sink*]. Oh yes, I believe you.

WACKA. He has. We just bin sittin' here waiting for you to get home.

MUM. Don't crawl to me. You'd stick up for him if he was paralytic.

> [*She fills jug, her back to them. A pause.* ALF *and* WACKA *exchange a "try-it-on" glance.*

[10]

WACKA [*tentatively*]. You look real nice tonight, Dot. You look nice in that getup.

MUM. You shut up, you old cow. [*But a moment later*] Want a cuppa cocoa?

WACKA. Nup.

MUM [*indifferently*]. All right. Well, if nobody else'll have any I can't be bothered makin' it for myself. [*At sink.*] Thought you was gunna do all them dishes for me after tea.

ALF. Oh, leave 'em. Leave 'em.

MUM. Yeah, leave 'em. I know who'll end up doin' 'em and it won't be you.

ALF. Don't take no notice of her. I know when she comes home a bit shirty, I know. Lose at the Housie-Housie, love?

MUM. I wasn't at the Housie-Housie. I was at the Euchre. And I won.

ALF. Bloody gambling. Still puttin' the kid through Uni, 'aven't got two bob to rub together and she's bloody gambling. The whole bloody country's living beyond its income. Look at Hughie's clothes. Clothes! What'd I know about clothes when I was his age?

MUM. He's got one suit and one sports outfit and he bought 'em out of his own money he earned drivin' the taxi for 'is mate in the weekend.

[*A pause.*

ALF [*a long, satirical stare at her*]. Well! Well! That's a turnup for the books, that is.

MUM. What is?

ALF. You stickin' up for him all of a sudden.

MUM. Drink yr beer.

ALF. Clothes and cameras, all Hughie thinks of.

MUM. He's got one camera.

ALF. Yeah, and all his money goes on it. The whole bloody
country's living beyond its income. Like that bloody little
jumped-up Pom in the lift today. Thinks 'e's Christmas
in 'is suede shoes and 'is little 'at with the feather in it
and his yeller vest, he's only a little clerk prob'ly; but do
they turn it on? *Do* they? And why? That's what I
want to know. Why? Why does he look at me as if I'm
a bad smell and he's the bloody ants pants, 'e's not worth
tuppence. He's not. He's not worth tuppence. I wouldn't
wipe me——

MUM [*from sink*] Alf——

ALF. Boots on 'im. 'Ow much did you win?

MUM. Two bob.

ALF. Two bob. And 'ow much did you lose last time?

MUM [*coming to stand over him*]. How much did you waste
on beer tonight?

ALF. You can see the bottles. Two bottles. If a man can't
spend a few bloody bob on a coupla bottles of beer——

MUM. And how long was you on it before the pubs shut?

ALF. Now listen, Dot——

MUM. Alf. It's bloody this and bloody that every two
seconds. I know how much you've had when you get to
this bloody stage.

ALF. Listen, love. [*Puts his arm up around her waist.*] It's
only a bit of a warmup.

[12]

MUM. I'll give you warmup.

ALF. Now, Dot——

MUM. All right, I know. I don't have to look at the calendar.
You can go the whole year without hardly touchin' a drop
and up comes April——

WACKA [*suddenly, into his beer*]. Oh to be in England now
that April's here.

ALF. England? Bugger England. I'm a bloody Australian,
mate, and it's because I'm a bloody Australian that I'm
gettin' on the grog. It's Anzac Day this week, that's my
day, that's the old digger's day——

MUM. You can old digger y'self to bed.

ALF [*a sudden sting*]. You bloodiwell leave me alone. [*They
glare at each other.*] You leave me alone. Yr always pretty
quick off the mark when it's me.

MUM. Well?

ALF. Well, y'mind yr ps and qs in front of the boy lately.
[*She moves to the sink without speaking. He follows her.*
Ah! Got her on the soft spot. Come on. Tell a man.
Let a man into the secret. What's the matter with Hughie?
What's the matter with him all of a sudden? He's the same
kid he always was. Well?

MUM. Shut up, Alf.

ALF. I won't shut up. [*They have suddenly quietened.*] I
want to know.
[*They face each other with the special deep hostility
of people who have been a long time married.*

MUM. Want to know what?

WACKA [*quietly*]. She's right, Alf. Everythink's right.

[13]

ALF. She watches him. I've seen her. When he's in the room she just watches him all the time. Hardly says a word.

MUM [*biting*]. I might if he said somethink to me——

ALF. Why's she got a snout on Hughie? What's he done?

MUM. Oh don't ask me. Wacka knows. He's noticed it.

ALF. Have you two been talkin' about my boy behind his back? Criticise, criticise.

MUM. Oh, of course you weren't, a minute ago, his clothes, his camera——

ALF. That's different. Hughie and me understand each other. I know you two buggers sittin' 'ere swillin' afternoon tea every day, mag, mag, mag——

WACKA [*meekly*]. I haven't said a word, Alf. Haven't said a word.

ALF. She's got some bee in her bonnet. [*He turns on her again.*] Well? [*She shrugs, moves away. Impatiently* ALF *turns to* WACKA.] Well?

WACKA [*hesitates, then*]. Kids change.

MUM. They don't have to change that much. Get home, Wacka, yr landlady'll be worryin'.

[WACKA *stands.*

ALF. 'Is landlady can mind her own bizness for once. Siddown, Wack.

[WACKA *sits.*

This is our last bottle. We're gunna finish this bottle. [ALF *begins to pour beer, looking up at* MUM.] And don' you worry about my young Hughie. He's all right.

[MUM *turns back to sink.* ALF *and* WACKA *lift glasses and drink.*

[14]

[*Lights on kitchen scene fade.*
[*Voices are heard outside sleepout section.*
[*From the darkness comes* JAN'S *voice.*

JAN. I hate them, hate them, hate them. How dare they?

[*Light in bedroom flicks on.* JAN *has hurried into the room.* HUGHIE *stands at door, hand on switch.*

HUGHIE [*laughing*]. Sit down and stop talking!

JAN. I'm furious. I hate them. How dare they dictate to me?

HUGHIE [*coming into room*]. You can't hate your parents. [*Grins.*] Hey—we're here.

[*They stand and look at each other, suddenly nervous. He moves towards her; she deftly avoids him, looks around the room.*

JAN. This your room? Isn't it gorgeous? So tiny.

HUGHIE [*slight chip on shoulder*]. Oh? It's all right.

JAN [*at window*]. Marvellous! You could almost touch the house next door.

HUGHIE. Haven't you got any neighbours?

JAN. We've the most gorgeous trees all around, one doesn't even notice them.

HUGHIE. Sit down.

JAN. On the bed? What if your mother comes in?

HUGHIE. Wouldn't matter. [*She sits as he throws cushions together for her. A moment of silence. He stands nearby, edgy, trying to drum up some social grace.*] Um—sorry I can't offer you a drink. Cigarette?

JAN. Thanks.

HUGHIE [*as he lights it*]. It is cramped, isn't it? I've been at the family to buy a new home, but they're that

[15]

conservative. It's pretty terrible when you want to bring anyone.

JAN. Hughie, you don't have to apologise.

HUGHIE. I'm not apologising. How were they dictating to you?

JAN. Oh, being late every night, all that jazz. My mother has a special telephone accent, it's so damned AFFECTED! God, she's a snob. Daddy's not so bad, but oh brother, my mother! Hughie—you are, you know. The very best thing that ever happened to me.

HUGHIE. Here we go. Society renegade finds peace in arms of proletariat.

JAN. Don't send me up, Hughie, please.

HUGHIE. Well, don't you patronise me.

JAN. Me——? When did I ever——?

HUGHIE. My dear, you could almost TOUCH the house next door, where I live we have trees all around, nothing so vulgar as a human being in sight.

JAN [gently]. It was being here—alone with you. I was just making conversation.

HUGHIE. Pretty bloody funny conversation. [They both smoke furiously, annoyed. He quietens. A pause. Gently he kisses her.] Why'd you want to come so much?

JAN. Now don't start.

HUGHIE. Don't start what?

JAN. That tired old sex stuff. I've had enough of that with the grade-one morons in my own set. I thought you'd be different.

HUGHIE. What, the virile, uncouth proletariat?

JAN. I thought your *values* would be different. I'm sick of elegant young men talking of tapered shoes and Jags

[16]

and MGs, in fact I'm sick of everybody in our mob, everybody.

HUGHIE. She did upset you.

JAN [*quickly*]. I'm glad I made you bring me, Hughie. It's lovely to see what they're like inside, these gorgeous quaint little houses——

HUGHIE. Your mother didn't want you to come here, did she?

JAN. My mother is a snob. [*At bedside table*] This the camera you're going to use? Isn't it . . . [*tails away*] gorgeous?

HUGHIE. What does she know about me?

JAN. Nothing. [*Quietly; dropping all pretence*] Hughie, I get so miserable. I told her weeks ago you were the most exciting thing ever, how we'd met through the Uni paper, how we were going to cook up the Anzac Day jazz, my words, your pictures—— [*She hesitates.*]

HUGHIE. And——?

JAN. She just happened to ask if she knew your family . . . You see, she took it absolutely for granted it would be one of our crowd. When I mentioned where you lived——

HUGHIE. She hit the roof, I suppose.

JAN. Hasn't come down *yet*. We've been fighting ever since.

HUGHIE. What does she think I am, some kind of village idiot?

JAN. Hughie, I want you to do something brave for me. Come up to our house for a weekend.

HUGHIE. Are you serious?

JAN. They'll only have to meet you, I know they'll fall,

[17]

they couldn't resist that honest, wonderful face—and your nice manners. Hughie, it's true, you're as well-mannered as any of the social crowd I've ever gone round with.

HUGHIE. I couldn't come up to your place.

JAN. Why not? We've often had—[*checks herself*] well, we have had boys up for weekends before.

HUGHIE [*unhappily*]. Oh.

JAN. Last year. [*Laughing.*] That was my Yacht Club phase. [*Looks at him.*] Hughie, you're not the very first boy I ever met.

HUGHIE. All right for them. I'd use the wrong knife or wrong fork or do something wrong. I'd disgrace you.

JAN. Those things don't worry me.

HUGHIE. They don't here. Now. In theory.

JAN. You've got to make an effort.

HUGHIE [*hesitates, then*]. No. No, I couldn't. I'm just not sure of myself.

JAN. But you can't stay here burrowed down in your own class all your life. If you get a profession, go out in the world, you'll have to learn to mix with all kinds of people.

HUGHIE. That's what I'm afraid of.

JAN. Afraid? I'll help you! Promise. [*He shakes his head. A pause.*] It does worry you, doesn't it?

HUGHIE. You're dead right, it does. Mahleesh.

JAN. Huh?

HUGHIE. Mahleesh. Expression Dad brought back from the Middle East. "Never mind." "Forget it." [*Suddenly serious*] Hey—did I hear you say—CLASS?

JAN. Yes, you did. [*Turning on him*] And you're not going

[18]

to tell me there's no such thing here. That's one of our myths.

HUGHIE [*uneasily*]. I've never thought about it.

JAN. That's not true, Hughie, it worries you every minute of the day. And you're right. [*Very dogmatic*] I don't know any girl, any friend of mine who's ever married or gone out with or even MET a boy from—well, round here.

HUGHIE. Well, no. [*Then realises implication.*]

JAN [*triumphantly*]. We marry the people we mix with and we mix with our own class. Australia, the great democracy. Wow!

HUGHIE [*quietly*]. *We* met. Because I'm at Uni. A—well, a—[*manages to say it*] a working-class kid. At Uni.

JAN. OK, they dole out bursaries. It only covers your fees. Your parents still have to battle, now don't they, to get you through, buy your books, clothe you, feed you—— Oh, they must have been wonderful.

HUGHIE. Ah, the proud peasant classes! Jan, my parents would bore you to tears.

JAN. I don't believe it.

HUGHIE [*quietly*]. I was lying about us getting a new house. We couldn't afford a new house. They don't want one. They *like* it here!

JAN. But that's why I came. To see what produced Hughie Cook.

HUGHIE. But, Jan, you couldn't bear it! The conversations in this house! [*Does his parents*] Avea cuppa tea, luv, avea cuppa tea, I don't wanta cuppa tea, all right, don't avea bloody cuppa tea!

[*They fall back on the bed, laughing.*

[19]

JAN. I'd love to meet them.

HUGHIE. No, you wouldn't. [*He turns abruptly away from her.*]

[*She watches him a moment.*

JAN. Hughie . . . You never talk about them. That's the first time. Don't you like them?

HUGHIE [*shrugging*]. That's a funny question, isn't it?

JAN. You disapprove of me attacking my parents. Yes, you do. And yet . . . What is it?

HUGHIE. Nothing. They drive me mad sometimes. They're so—so—— [*He stops, seems to be feeling for words.*]

JAN. Well? They're so what?

HUGHIE. Do you know I never can find the word? Somewhere in the back of my mind there's one word, one word that sums up all they represent, all I can't stand. But I can never find it.

JAN [*gently*]. This Anzac Day story—wouldn't have anything to do with them, would it?

HUGHIE. I don't dig.

JAN. You get so burned-up about it. I don't know anybody who takes it so seriously. [*Pause.*] *Why* do you?

HUGHIE. Why do I? I wonder. [*A pause.*] I can't stand waste. Waste of lives, waste of men. That whole thing— Anzac—Gallipoli—was a waste. Certainly nothing to glorify. [*Impatiently*] God, there's been another war since then! Dozens of wars everywhere, thousands of lousy little victories and defeats to forget. But they go on and on about this one year after year, as though it really was something.

JAN. And so young Hughie's going to ride in on his white horse——

HUGHIE. Don't laugh at me. This time last year, all the week before, I watched him getting worse and worse. I thought, I won't go. I won't observe it any more. But I did. When it came to the point I did. Well, that was the last time. This time I'm going to celebrate Anzac Day my way, with my feelings, my photos from my camera, on paper, in print. Even if it rubbishes absolutely and completely all I've been brought up on, that's what I'm going to do.

JAN. Save it—I've already joined. I'll write you the best story you've ever seen, Hughie. But those photos will have to be magnificent.

HUGHIE. Oh, think I can't do it? [*He grabs up camera.*] This is how I get my kicks.

JAN. And this is how I get mine. [*Leans over and kisses him gently.*]

HUGHIE. Do you like me a bit? [*She nods.*] Gee, I wish——

JAN. What do you wish, Hughie Cook——?

HUGHIE. *Can* we like each other? Would it ever work?

JAN. Why shouldn't it? [*He shrugs.*] Oh, my mother.

HUGHIE. Not just her. My people too. The whole set-up.

JAN. *I* want it to work. I do, Hughie.

HUGHIE. Then we'll make it work.

[*They are suddenly embracing hungrily and fall across the bed. She pushes him away.*

JAN. Hughie! [*They struggle.*] Hughie!! [*They struggle.*] Hughie!!!

HUGHIE. Now don't go all moral on me.

JAN. I just want to be sensible.

HUGHIE. Sensible? CRIKEY!

> [*He reaches up, flicks off bedlamp.*
> [*Lights on bedroom scene fade.*
> [*Lights up in kitchen.* MUM *has been groping in dresser drawer and cardigan pockets.*

MUM. Got a shilling for the meter? I'm right out.

ALF. I'm broke.

WACKA [*feeling in pockets*]. Got two sixpences.

MUM. That's a great help. [*She moves away.*] Hughie might have some in his drawer.

ALF. Don't go rattin' the kid's drawer. He's a growing lad, y'never know what y' might find.

MUM. I'd better not find anything.

> [*She goes across lounge room, switching on light. Stops halfway across room, spots magazines and papers thrown on floor, starts tidying up and knocks ashtray over.*
> [*The light in the bedroom snaps on,* HUGHIE'S *hand on it. One arm is still around* JAN. *They both listen.*

HUGHIE. Dad.

> [*In an instant they are apart,* JAN *adjusting her sweater, patting back her hair,* HUGHIE *putting pillow and cushions back in right place.*
> [MUM *throws papers on couch, crosses, opens door to* HUGHIE'S *room.*
> [JAN *is sitting primly on edge of bed.* HUGHIE *stands at cupboard at other end of room.*

[22]

HUGHIE. This is the camera . . . [*Turns innocently to face door.*] Oh . . . [*At sight of his mother, closes up.*] Oh. Hullo.

> [MUM *is a little taken aback.* JAN *rises, realises she has kicked her shoes off.*

MUM. I'm sorry. Didn't hear y' come in. [*She eyes* JAN *over.*]

HUGHIE. We just got here. [JAN *is trying to slip foot into shoe.*] This is Jan. Jan Castle, she's at Uni. Jan, this is my mother.

JAN. I'm very glad to meet you, Mrs. Cook.

MUM. Yes. Well, you'd better come into the lounge.

HUGHIE. Oh—Jan wasn't staying.

JAN. But I'd love to stay. I've been so wanting to meet Hughie's parents.

HUGHIE. But—[*embarrassed*] Dad'll be going to bed, won't he?

MUM. Dunno about that, he looks right for the night to me.

HUGHIE (*to* JAN). It's a bit late, isn't it?

MUM. What's the matter with you? [*To* JAN] You'll have a cuppa tea, won't you?

JAN. Please don't go to any trouble.

MUM. It's no trouble. Come on.

HUGHIE [*grudgingly*]. Well, all right.

MUM. Oh, got a shilling for the meter? [*To* JAN] Gas meter. Drive you mad.

HUGHIE [*feeling in pocket*]. Sorry, I'm flat.

JAN. Here. [*Pulls some loose notes and silver from her pocket.*] There's sure to be . . . Yes, there.

[23]

MUM. Oh, I wouldn't dream——

JAN. Go on.

MUM. Well . . . Hughie can give it to you tomorrow. [*Takes money.*] Thanks.

ALF [*yelling from kitchen*]. Where the bloody hell are you?

MUM [*yelling back*]. Awright, don't get orf yr bike!

> [*She goes.* JAN *stares after her.* HUGHIE *grabs* JAN'S *arm.*]
>
> [HUGHIE *switches bedroom light off at second switch near lounge door. They go through to lounge,* MUM *ahead.*]

HUGHIE. Don't take too much notice of Dad. I mean, if he's a bit . . . [*He is nervous, on edge.*]

MUM [*shaking cushions on chair*]. Siddown and take the weight off yr feet.

> [JAN *sits,* HUGHIE *perches on arm of chair next to her.*]

ALF. For Christ's sake, Mother, come on——!

MUM. We're in here.

> [ALF *and* WACKA *come towards lounge, armed with glasses and bottle.*]

ALF. Where've y'been? Takes y'long enough to get a bob, don't it? Thought you'd gone to the dunny and fell in.

> [*He stands in doorway and sees* JAN. HUGHIE *is mortified.* MUM *looks daggers at* ALF.]

MUM. Hughie's brought a young lady—from the University——

> [ALF *has whipped bottle behind him and is passing it back to* WACKA. WACKA *is on tiptoe, peering over* ALF'S *shoulder.*]

ALF. Yes. Well, that's real nice. [*His elbow connects with* WACKA'S *stomach,* WACKA *withdraws to kitchen, puts bottle and glasses down.* ALF *hitches up his trousers, comes into lounge with an attempt at dignity and sobriety.*] Any friend of Hughie's is a friend of ours.

HUGHIE. This is Jan Castle.

ALF. Pleased t'meetcher. [*He has approached her, is not sure whether to shake hands or not, finally doesn't, turns to* MUM.] Well, Mother, aren't you gunna give the young lady a cuppa tea?

JAN. I won't have one, thanks. [*Realises this may sound rude.*] Really. I hardly ever drink tea.

MUM. Don't drink tea. What do you drink?

JAN. Coffee mostly.

ALF. Bad as Hughie. Hughie's startin' on that. See them black rings under 'is eyes? That's coffee.

HUGHIE. Sit down, Dad.

ALF [*sitting*]. Well, don't have anything to drink if you don't want to.

> [WACKA'S *head has come tentatively through door. Spotting* JAN *he hastily withdraws.* MUM *sits.*

JAN [*offering cigarettes around*]. Cigarette?

ALF. I've got the makin's.

JAN [*to* HUGHIE]. Darling, light me.

> [HUGHIE *whips out matches, lights her cigarette.* ALF *and* MUM *exchange a glance at the "darling".*
>
> [*A silence.*

ALF. Well . . . [*Looks around with a large, uncomfortable smile.*]

> [*A silence.* JAN *smokes.* HUGHIE *is miserable.*

HUGHIE. Jan drove me home.

ALF. You got a car?

JAN. It's the family's. I'm allowed to have it if Daddy's not using it.

[*A pause.*

ALF. You English?

JAN. Who me? [*Laughs, then in speech perilously close to their own*] No, I'm a dinky-di Aussie.

ALF. Aussie? You kids aren't bloody Aussies.

MUM. Alf. . . .

ALF. Look at Hughie. Look at his clothes. He's done up like a Yank. I dunno . . . what's happenin' to the country? When I was your age we was Australian and proud of it.

HUGHIE. Oh, don't start.

ALF. You kids, you aren't happy unless you're copyin' the Yanks, wearin' Yank clothes, singin' Yank songs, rock an' ruddy roll. [*To* MUM] I tell you . . . me and Wack, we're the last of the Australians. When we're gone, when blokes our age are gone, what'll you have? A stinkin' lot of imitation Yanks, the whole damn country's goin' down the drain. . . .

MUM. Why don't you say a few words?

JAN. Don't you think, Mr. Cook, I mean all this change, don't you think it's good for us? We're not half so insular.

ALF [*to* HUGHIE]. What does that mean?

HUGHIE [*bitingly*]. It means we're beginning to grow up——

ALF. Chris', look who's talkin'.

HUGHIE. As a nation. We're not so isolated any more. The Europeans here—dozens of different nationalities—

[26]

they're giving us something new—cutting right across the old Australian stiff-neck.

[*His mother watches alarmed as his speech seems to turn into an attack.*

ALF. What's 'e talkin' about?

HUGHIE. All that old eyewash about national character's a thing of the past. Australians are this, Australians are that, Australians make the greatest soldiers, the best fighters, it's all rubbish. [*His father is about to cut in.* HUGHIE *finishes in a rush*] The Europeans here force us to see that all people are pretty much the same, and that's the best thing that ever happened to this country, maybe the next generation won't be so one-eyed.

[ALF *looks up quickly.*

MUM [*embarrassed, tries to cover up*]. Gets it from his father. Talk.

JAN. I think Hughie's quite right, you know. [*They turn to her warily. She smiles, hauls the conversation on.*] Take the migrants, as Hughie says. Look at the difference they've made to our eating habits.

ALF. I still eat three meals a day. Breakfast, dinner and tea.

JAN. I meant their restaurants.

MUM. Restaurants? You can't get a good cuppa tea any more. Everything's expresso coffee. Gives me heartburn

ALF. That's it! Poms, Yanks and bloody I-ties.

HUGHIE [*turning to him*]. If you can't discuss it intelligently——

ALF. Oh! [*Pukka accent, to* MUM] Oh, I say, Mother, sit up, old girl, we're going to have an intelligent

[27]

discussion. An intelligent discussion. [*To* HUGHIE] Well, go ahead. Go ahead, *old man*, go ahead.

HUGHIE [*tightly*]. Let's skip it, shall we?

> [*An uncomfortable pause.* ALF *relaxes a little, feeling he has scored a point, and turns to* JAN.

ALF. Where you from?

JAN. Here.

ALF. Here?

JAN. Sydney.

ALF. What part?

JAN. Roseville Chase.

ALF. Oh. North Shore.

JAN. What work do you do, Mr. Cook?

ALF. I'm a lift driver. War wound.

JAN. Oh?

HUGHIE. Alamein.

ALF. Don't ask me to show you it. [*Laughs, suddenly belches.*] 'Scuse me.

JAN [*quickly, to cover* HUGHIE'S *embarrassment*]. What a charming little place you have here. I was just saying to Hughie——

MUM. Dad's prob'ly not feeling too good.

ALF. Ay?

MUM. He's just been having a talk with an old friend.

ALF. Now look—now look, I'm not ashamed to admit I've been having a few drinks——

JAN [*to the rescue*]. That's just what I'd like. I really honestly don't feel like a cup of tea but I'd love something stronger.

[28]

ALF. Good on yer. What'll y'have?

JAN. I don't mind. Can I have a Scotch?

ALF. Ay?

JAN [*immediately apologises*]. Oh—if you don't have any——

HUGHIE. We've probably only got beer.

JAN. Well, I don't care for it usually, but [*big smile at* DAD] I'd love one.

ALF. Wacka! [*To* JAN] Youse'll be sweet.

[WACKA *puts his head in.*

Well, what's the matter with you? Come on.

[WACKA *starts to enter, empty-handed.*

No, no! Where's the stuff? Go and get it—and a couple of extra glasses. You'll find another bottle in the back of the cupboard——

MUM. I thought that was the last one.

ALF [*yells*]. Behind the Corn Flakes packet. [*To* JAN] Y'always want to get the big size, they'd hide anything.

JAN [*to* MUM]. You must be very proud of Hughie.

MUM [*embarrassed*]. Oh . . . you know.

ALF. The Uni's made a lot of difference to Hughie. Smartened up 'is ideas.

HUGHIE. My public.

ALF. Oh? You still 'ere? Thought you'd gone to bed. [*To* JAN] Thinks he's real sophisticated now, Hughie. [*Grunts.*] Prob'ly is too.

JAN. I like him because he isn't. Well, not too.

ALF. Get out, he's bright, Hughie——

HUGHIE. Oh—— Come off it.

ALF. He's good at his studies, isn't he?

JAN. I didn't say he wasn't.

[29]

ALF. Hughie's all right. He's all right. Gets a bit carried away but he's a good kid. [*He turns to* JAN.] I wisht I'd had half his chances. I do. I didn't ever get to any Universities. The University of hard knocks, that's all I ever had.

HUGHIE. I don't know what you're complaining about. You've done all right, haven't you?

ALF. Of course I done all right. [*To* JAN] I'm in a very good job, you know. This lift-driving, it's only temporary, see—[*his family is surprised*] and I've got a very good chance of getting into something better soon.

JAN. That's nice.

ALF. Better job, much better pay, and that won't be hard to take, putting him through. [*Jerking his head at* HUGHIE] Our staff superintendent, see Mr. Wilson, he's a very nice chap, nothing stuckup. Well, they're buildin' a new plant out of town, and they need a kind of supervisor out there, see.

JAN. Oh, that sounds quite important. That'd be an executive position, wouldn't it?

ALF. That's it, that's what it'll be. Kind of an executive position. [MUM *and* HUGHIE *are half-embarrassed, half-astonished.*] You'd have to look after the plant and prob'ly do a bit of maintenance. Well, I've always been good on that. Machines, like. Always had a bit of a kink about that sort of thing. Well, that's the kind of bloke they want. So when I see it advertised, I got hold of Mr. Wilson and I said to him, What do you want to go advertising for? You've got a good man right here and you don't know it, so we had a bit of a mag and I look pretty right.

HUGHIE. Dad . . .

ALF. He said he'd put in a good word for me, see.

MUM [*flatly*]. There's nothing definite, is there?

ALF. Ay?

MUM. The way you talk——

ALF. Of course it's definite. I told you about it a month ago when I spoke to him.

MUM. Yeah. You told me.

ALF. Well?

[MUM *and* HUGHIE *exchange a glance.*

MUM. Aren't you a bit old?

ALF. Arr, go on. They want someone with a bit of sense.

MUM [*dubiously*]. Hmmm!

ALF. Well, I keep reminding him, every time he gets in the lift I have a bit of a go at him, see. Well, he would've told me if they were gettin' someone else, would he? He says they're lookin' into it. They're lookin' into it. These things take time. Of course it's definite. [*To* JAN, *indicating* MUM] Gawd, talk about a wet blanket.

JAN. Well, I hope it comes off for you, Mr. Cook. It sounds very nice.

ALF. It'll come off, all right, it'll come off.

[WACKA *comes back, loaded with bottles and glasses.* [*Springing up*] That's it, Wack.

[WACKA *has put things on table, stands looking sheepish.*

Wacka, this is a young lady friend of Hughie's. Miss— er—Miss—this is Wacka Dawson. Wack—Miss——

HUGHIE. Castle.

JAN. Jan.

ALF. Miss Jane Castle.

WACKA [*shyly*]. 'Ow y'goin'? [*He opens bottle, starts pouring.*]

ALF. Wack and me are old mates. At the war together.

JAN. Which one?

ALF. Fair go. Second.

HUGHIE [*laughing*]. Think I was a late baby or something?

ALF. A man ain't that old. Wacka was in the first though.
Wack's a real old friend of the family. Wack goes back a
long way, don't you, Wack?

WACKA [*laughs*]. Yeah. Yeah. [*Then, embarrassed at his
own presumption, mumbles*] The Dawsons and the Cooks
was always mates. They was always mates.

ALF. Wacka's been in both shows, you was in the Fourteen-
Eighteen and the Second one, wasn't you, Wack? He
was at World War One with my Dad and World War
Two with me. That's a record, isn't it, eh? That's a good
record.

JAN. My word.

　　　　[*A pause. They seem to have come to a dead stop.*

HUGHIE [*making conversation*]. Wacka—I've been trying to
work it out for years. Come clean now. How old are
you?

　　　　　　　　　　[WACKA *proffers glass to* HUGHIE.

WACKA. 'Ave a beer.

HUGHIE [*taking glasses from tray and giving one to* JAN].
You're not going to wriggle out of it that way. How old
is he, Dad?

ALF. Search me.

HUGHIE. Wack——?

WACKA. I dunno. [*Grins, shrugs.*]

MUM. He's lost count.

HUGHIE. You must have some idea.

WACKA. I dunno. [*Pause. They all look at him.*] What I did I put me age up to get into the First World War and down to get into the Second.

ALF. Gawd, you must be old.

MUM. He wouldn't know. True. He's got no one to keep count for him, have you, Wack? Now, go on, have you? [*To* JAN] 'E's never got married. 'E's never 'ad no one.

WACKA. I've had youse.

ALF. You said it, Wack. What d'y'mean 'e never had no one? We bin mates for years. I've looked after him, haven't I, Wack? I seen 'im through. [*To* JAN] What I c'n work out, my old man seen 'im through the first show, I looked after him all through the last lot. And did he take some lookin' after? Two left feet. No fingers, all thumbs.

HUGHIE. He's a good barman anyway. Mind if we get this down.

ALF. Jeez. Sorry.

MUM [*indicating* ALF]. He can talk the leg off an iron pot.

JAN [*smiles at* MUM]. Hughie is like his father.

ALF. Hughie? Talk? You see that turn he put on just now? He useter talk like that all the time once. Of course, nobody ever listened. But he's bin quietenin' down lately. [*To* HUGHIE] Why don't you rave on sometimes like you useter?

[33]

HUGHIE [*abruptly*.] Can't get a word in edgewise. Well ...
[*Lifts his glass.*]
        [ALF, WACK *and* JAN *follow suit.* MUM *is not drinking*.
ALF. Good 'ealth.
JAN. Skoal. [ALF, WACKA, HUGHIE *drink.* JAN *has glass to her lips when——*]
MUM. You say you was drivin'?
JAN. Pardon?
MUM. You've got to drive home, haven't you?
JAN. Why, yes.
HUGHIE [*irritably*]. Drink up. Go on.
ALF [*when* JAN *hesitates*]. Go on, miss. Get it down. [*To* MUM] What's the matter with you? She's only having one. You're only having one, aren't you?
MUM. Y'know what it says on the wiless.
                                    [*A slight pause.*
JAN [*battling to keep even-tempered*]. No. What does it say on the wireless?
MUM [*heavily*]. When y'r drivin' don't drink. When yr drink'n' don't drive.
HUGHIE. Mum, for God's sake.
ALF. Arr, get orf 'er back, the girl's only walked into the place and you start.
JAN. Mrs. Cook's right, really.
HUGHIE. Drink your beer and——
JAN. No really. But do you think just one little sip——?
MUM. I didn't mean to make a song and dance about it.
JAN [*takes a mouthful, puts glass down, beams at* MUM. HUGHIE *is annoyed, with both of them.* ALF *and* WACKA *look uncomfortable,* MUM *disapproves*]. There—— Now,
[34]

what were we talking about? I know, Mr. Dawson's age.

ALF. Bugger 'is age. 'Scuse me, miss.

JAN. But it is very interesting. He went through the Second World War with you——

ALF. I've known Wacka all my life. I grew up knowin' 'im. That man—[*pointing to* WACKA *rhetorically*] that man practically brung me up. 'E looked after me when me old mother was battlin' in the twenties, on her own. Me old man never came back, see, from the first one. [*An almost professional air of grief has automatically appeared in him.*]

JAN. Oh, I'm sorry.

ALF. 'E was done in by the Turk [*a pause*]—Gallipoli.

    [JAN *sits very still, tense, on the edge of her chair. Slowly she puts down her glass.*

JAN [*softly*]. Gallipoli? You mean . . . [*to* WACKA] you were there? [WACKA *nods.* JAN *turns to* HUGHIE.] We've found one! Why didn't you tell me?

HUGHIE [*uneasily*]. Didn't even think of it——

    [JAN *is almost bursting with excitement.*

JAN [*to* WACKA]. But this is wonderful. You must tell me all about it.

WACKA. All about what?

JAN. Hasn't Hughie told you——?

ALF. Told us what?

HUGHIE. Jan——

JAN. We're both on the Uni paper now. I write for it, Hughie takes the pictures. We're doing a feature on Anzac Day, for the next issue——

ALF. Well! That's nice. That's real nice. We're pretty

strong on Anzac Day in this house—because of the old Dad, see. We always keep it up, don't we, Hughie? Hughie's been to the dawn service and the march with me every year since he was that high.

JAN. Yes, well——

ALF. And yr writin' a story about it? Gawd, that Hughie, he wouldn't tell y'nothin'. Well . . . you've come to the right place. If you want to know something about the old diggers, you've come to the right place. [*Expansively*] What do you want to know?

JAN [*impatiently*]. You weren't there.
      [*She gets up quickly, goes to* WACKA. ALF *is offended.*
Mr. Dawson, you've no idea how keen I am to get the real, the authentic feel of the thing, to contrast it with what's come after. I wonder if you would help me. This is what I have in mind.
      [WACKA *has been edging away, embarrassed.*

ALF. He can't tell y'anythin'. He never opens 'is mouth about it.

WACKA. I dunno nothin'.

JAN. I'm sure you're just being modest, Mr. Dawson, and that's exactly what I want. [*She has him in corner chair, hemmed in.*] Now I have a theory about this. As you know there's been more rubbish written about Anzac Day than about any other subject in Australia. Now my feeling is that all the hot air comes from those who were never there and who just go on mouthing all the platitudes until they come to believe them themselves and——
      [HUGHIE *has glanced quickly at his father who has tried to follow* JAN *but has lost her.* HUGHIE *hurries across to* JAN.

[36]

HUGHIE. Jan, it's a bit late, isn't it?

JAN [*turning to him*]. What?

> [HUGHIE *takes her arm and gets her, in spite of herself, to her feet.*

HUGHIE. I've got some work to do before I go to bed—this can keep.

JAN. But, Hughie, it's so wonderful. [*To* WACKA *who sits bolt upright, scared, staring at her*] I've never met one, you see, there can't be a lot of them left now, can there? I've been wanting—ever since Hughie got me interested —I've been wanting to talk, to question——

HUGHIE. Jan! [*She stops, turns to him.*] Knock it off, eh?

> [*She looks past him to* MUM *and* DAD *sitting stiffly looking at her and begins to get the message.*

JAN. Oh. Well, if you really think——

HUGHIE. Yes I do.

JAN. Well, when may I?

HUGHIE. Talk about it tomorrow. Everyone's tired. [*Appeals to others*] It is late, isn't it? This girl keeps such crazy hours.

MUM. Well, I don't. I've got to get up and get them two off tomorrow.

JAN. May I come again? [*She looks eagerly from* MUM *to* ALF, *is both sincere and patronising at the same time and* HUGHIE *could kill her.*] May I, please?

MUM [*uncomfortably*]. It's all right with me.

JAN. Oh, thank you.

MUM [*getting up*]. I think Hughie'd better get y'off home. I bin out and I'm tired anyway.

[37]

JAN [*piqued*]. Oh, I'm sorry. I didn't realise you'd been out. I thought you'd been home all evening [*too sweetly*] in the kitchen.

MUM. If I'd been home all evening these two wouldn't be the cotcases they are. I bin at the Euchre.

JAN. The what?

MUM. With the girls. Playin' Euchre.

ALF. She won two bob. Turnup for the books, she usually comes 'ome half a quid behind.

JAN. But how interesting. You don't like drink but gambling's OK. Gorgeous!

HUGHIE [*tugging* JAN *away*]. Well, we'll be getting along now—I'll see Jan out. Say Goodnight.

JAN. Goodnight. . . .

[HUGHIE *charges out of room pushing* JAN *ahead of him and carefully closing door behind him. For a second or two nobody in the lounge moves. Then* WACKA *pipes up.*

WACKA. She's orf 'er nut.

ALF [*nods slowly*]. What was it she was sayin' to you?

WACKA. I dunno.

ALF. Neither do I. Never understood a word of it. [*Turns to* MUM] What do you reckon?

MUM. She wears too much lipstick.

[*Lights in lounge out. Lights up in* HUGHIE'S *room.* JAN *is sitting on bed, combing her hair.* HUGHIE *turns to her.*

HUGHIE. That wasn't funny.

JAN. What wasn't?

[38]

HUGHIE. Getting at them.

[*He turns away from her furiously. She rises, comes to him.*

JAN. Hughie? Are you cross with me?

HUGHIE. Yes. No. Not just you.

JAN [*gently*]. With them?

HUGHIE. With myself, for being—— [*Shrugs.*]

JAN. They're very nice, Hughie. Terribly nice.

HUGHIE. They're not. They're——

JAN. They're what?

HUGHIE. They're so—so—oh, I don't know.

JAN. They're themselves. They're honest.

HUGHIE. And so quaint?

JAN. I didn't mean to sound rude.

HUGHIE. Oh forget it. It's just—sometimes I feel myself getting farther and farther away from them.

JAN. Isn't that natural? You've left them miles behind and so you should, it's right that you should. That's what I admire in you.

HUGHIE. True?

JAN. True.

[*His arms are around her. He kisses her, a long, slow kiss. She moves away.*

I thought you said you had some study to do.

HUGHIE [*snapping mood*]. Half an hour before I go to bed. Every night!

JAN. You're made of iron. [*Kisses him again, lightly.*] I'm going home.

[39]

HUGHIE. I'll see you to the car. [*They start to go.*] Hey, why for God's sake did you mention that damned Anzac Day story.

JAN. Well, why not?

HUGHIE. I haven't said a word.

JAN. Hughie, really. You can be too soft.

HUGHIE. You kidding? If Dad sees it——

JAN [*a pause*]. Maybe you shouldn't have agreed to do it.

HUGHIE. I want to do it. It's what I believe.

JAN. Well, then . . .

[*He shakes his head, worried.*
Well?

HUGHIE. Come on.

[*They go out through outside door of his room.*
[*Lights up in kitchen.* WACKA *has gone.* MUM *is at sink drying glasses.* ALF *sits polishing his shoes. An electric jug is heating.*

ALF [*quietly*]. She was havin' a go at you, Mother.

MUM. If y'ask me she was havin' a go at all of us.

ALF. No. No. Wouldn't say that.

MUM. She sobered you up, I'll say that for her.

ALF. Poor old Wack. See poor old Wack when she had 'im in that chair?

MUM. What'd he shoot off for? I was gunna make 'im a cuppa tea.

ALF [*yawning*]. Gawd, Mum, you're a bugger for that tea.

MUM. You want one?

ALF. No, I don't. I'd've asked if I'd wanted a cuppa tea.

MUM. Don't start again.

[40]

ALF. Well, I'm tired. I don't wanta keep bein' asked if I wanta cuppa tea when I'm tired.

MUM. Well, go to bed, why don't you?

ALF. I don't *wanta* go to bed.

MUM. Oh. [*She stands dead still.*]

ALF. What's wrong?

MUM. I just remembered. [*Fishing it out of cardigan pocket*] She give me a bob for the meter and I didn't use it.

ALF [*grunts*]. She won't miss it.

> [*The electric jug begins to boil.* MUM *attends to it, begins to make tea. Her back is to* ALF. *He sits a moment, looks at her thoughtfully.*]

[*Tentatively*] Didn't know young Hughie had a girl.

MUM [*without turning around*]. Ay?

ALF. She his girl?

MUM. Who, her? She's not his girl.

ALF. How d'y'know?

MUM. 'E would've said.

ALF. Would 'e?

MUM [*turning to look at him over her shoulder*]. Well, he would've said somethink.

ALF. 'E hasn't bin saying too much lately.

MUM. Oh. Wakin' up, are you?

ALF. Wakin' up—what to?

> [MUM *has finished putting tea and hot water in pot, which she now covers with cosy and stands on mat. She turns to face him.*

[41]

MUM. I told you. Hughie's changin'. In fact, he's changed.

ALF. Oh, he's just growing up. A boy gets restless.

MUM. It's more than that. You saw him in there. You heard him, making his speech.

ALF. Oh, he's always talked like that.

MUM. No he hasn't. [*Struggling to express it*] Well, he has, but now it's different. Before it was just—letting off steam. Now it's personal. Directed at us.

ALF [*after staring up at her to digest this*]. Come 'ere, Dot. Siddown. [*She does so. He is quiet.*] That what you were gettin' at before? When Wacka was here? [*She nods.*] What is it, Dot?

MUM. Don't ask me 'cause you won't like what I say.

ALF. I am asking you, aren't I? What is it with Hughie?

MUM [*reluctantly*]. Oh, I dunno.

ALF. Go on. Get it off yr chest. [*She shakes her head impatiently, lips set hard.*] Well?

MUM [*suddenly*]. It's all this education, that's what it is.

ALF. Oh, go on with you.

MUM. All right.

ALF. We spent our whole life practically ever since he was born, makin' sure he'd have an education. What are you talkin' about, his education? It's his education that's making Hughie what he is.

MUM. That's just what I mean.

ALF [*in profound disgust*]. Arrr. . . .

MUM. All right. You know everything.

ALF. I know my own son.

[42]

MUM. Alf . . . [*Her tone fixes his attention.*]

ALF. Well, go on. Don't just sit there lookin' niggly. What?

MUM. He's my son too. I don't get round singing his praises, but he's my kid. [*Slight nod.*] It's all right for you. You and him always got on all right. When he was a kid and you'd roar at him about something, I'd watch him nearly howling because it was you tearin' him to shreds. [*Quietly*] I'd want to speak to him. But I could never speak to him. Hughie and me could never talk. [*She looks at him directly.*] That doesn't mean I don't—— [*She stops.*] He's my kid. And all I know is he looks at me sometimes as though I'm nothing, as though I'm just nothing. He's not the same.

ALF. He's the same to me. I never seen no difference in my son and I never will. He'll always be the same to me.

MUM. Have it your own way.

ALF. Right. Hughie's OK. Hughie's OK. Where's my cuppa tea?

MUM. Your——? [*She gets up, goes to pot, pours furiously, banging everything she touches, brings cup down and slams it in front of him.*] There, and you know what you can do with it.

ALF [*stirring sugar and mumbling*]. You make me sick, criticisin' the kid. Y'ought to be proud of him, like she said.

MUM. Don't drag her in.

ALF. Pick, pick, pick, why don't you leave the kid alone?

MUM. I never said nothin' to the kid.

[43]

ALF. No, y're not game to out with it and give 'im a piece of yr mind, y'drive me barmy instead.

MUM. Oh, shut up, Alf.

ALF [standing now and beginning to roar even more irritably than when he was drunk]. I—WILL—NOT—SHUT UP. You get orf my back. You think I'm not sick of havin' people on my back all day goin' up and down, up and down, up and down, pick, pick, pick, think they're God Almighty and treat you like a bitta furniture, I'm a bloody Australian and I'm as good as anybody gets in that lift——

MUM. How did that get into it?

ALF. Don't you go me. [He has worked himself into a fury again and is standing over her.] You can try my patience just so far, Dot, but you overstep the mark and I'll—I'll——

MUM [looking up at him unperturbed]. Y'll what?

ALF [flinging away from her]. Arr, why don't you leave a man alone?

> [He sits. She takes a mouthful of tea, looks down into cup as though suddenly wondering how and why she is drinking it, then gets up, takes cup to sink.

MUM. I'm getting ready for bed.

ALF [mumbling]. Get ready—and bugger you.

> [He sits, sulking. MUM makes sure gas is off, goes to their bedroom door, turns to him.

MUM. You let Hughie get his work done. Don't you start on him. [He doesn't answer.] You leave him alone.

ALF [turns slowly, eyes her coldly]. When did I ever stand in Hughie's light?

MUM. There's a cuppa tea there if he wants one. You better get to bed too.

> [*She goes.* ALF *sits still, staring at nothing. Then, shrugging it off, he gets up, takes cup and saucer to sink, refills cup, tries pot and slips a cosy over it to keep tea warm. Returning to table, he begins putting boot polish and brushes back into kit.*
>
> [HUGHIE *comes back to his bedroom, collects his books, and with a certain restlessness gets notepaper, etc., together. The moment before he switches the light out in his bedroom he looks about the room, a hard, critical look.*
>
> [*He moves into the main room and stands there alone a moment, looking up and about the whole room with a sudden excess of displeasure. Then with a shrug he moves into the kitchen.*

HUGHIE. Where is everybody?

ALF. Yr mother's going to bed. Wacka went home. [*Carefully*] She scared him.

HUGHIE. Who, Jan? [*He laughs a little unconvincingly, starts putting books on table, thumbing through exercise books, looking through pockets for Biro.*

ALF. There's a cuppa tea there.

HUGHIE. No thanks. [*He sits, finds place in book and is ready to begin work.*]

ALF. Where'd you pick her up?

HUGHIE. Mmm? [*Transfers his attention from book to* ALF.] Oh, she's in my year.

> [ALF *nods.* HUGHIE *goes back to work.*

ALF. Sure you won't 'ave a cuppa tea?

[45]

HUGHIE. No.

[*A break.*

ALF. I'll get it for you.

HUGHIE. Don't worry.

ALF. It's no trouble, son. Won't take half a sec.

HUGHIE. Don't feel like it, thanks.

[*A break.*

ALF. It's nice 'n' hot.

HUGHIE. Mmm?—Oh, no thanks.

ALF. Wouldn't take a minute. [*Impatiently*, HUGHIE *shakes his head.*] All right, I won't press you.

> [ALF *sits down, watches* HUGHIE. *Gradually all the resentment in him fades. His head a little on one side, he begins to smile, eyes fixed on his son at work.*

What are y' studyin' at tonight?

HUGHIE. Statistics.

> [HUGHIE *continues to work.* ALF *sits watching him with a smile that is part-envy, part-awe.*

ALF [*after a little while*]. You must be clever, Hughie.

> [HUGHIE *looks up, a little embarrassed. His father is sitting back contentedly, smiling at him.* HUGHIE *manages a smile, returns to his work. Another pause.*

What are y'gunna be, Hughie? I mean, what are y' studyin' for?

HUGHIE [*as patiently as he can*]. I've told you.

ALF. Yeah, but I mean—well, tell me.

HUGHIE. Well, there's different things I could qualify for, I'll get my Economics degree—[*grins*] I hope—and then —see what's going.

[46]

ALF. Oh. [*Thinks about this.*] Don't you wanta be anything special, you know, when you leave?

HUGHIE. You know me, I'd like to spend my life taking pictures—but what you want to do and what you've got to do, to earn a living, are two different things, aren't they?

ALF. Huh! You're tellin' *me* that. But—you'll have to make up yr mind sooner or later, won't you?

HUGHIE. I wish I could. I think I've always wanted to be educated for the sake of—— [*Breaks.*] Well, you always wanted me to—— [*He hesitates.*] So I did. Oh, I'm glad I did.

ALF. You still like goin' to University?

HUGHIE. I like it all right. Why shouldn't I?

ALF. It'll make a difference, you know, son. You kids to-day, you get everything. I wisht I'd had your chances. [*A pause.* HUGHIE *goes on working.* ALF *is looking dreamily into space now.*] I always wanted to be an engineer, did I ever tell you that? [HUGHIE *is about to signify that he has but refrains when he sees his father's mood.*] I useter muck around with cars and engines and that all the time when I was a kid. But in those days . . . well, the old Dad goin' off at the war and things bein' a bit hard—me Mum couldn't afford to do much for me, see. I had to get out and work. What work you could get. But I tell you some-th'n', son. Tell y' someth'n'. All through the depression I tried to study, orf me own bat. I used to go to the Muni-cipal Library to get the books 'cause it was free, like, technical books and that, I spent hours over 'em, years. [*Grunts.*] Fat lot of good they did me. [*He turns to*

[47]

HUGHIE [*quietly*]. I hope you do someth'n' good with yr study, son. We can't do much for you, we've got no money, but we always do what we can, you know that, don't you?

[HUGHIE *looks away, conscience stung.*

HUGHIE. Yes, Dad. I know. [*A pause. He tries to work.*]

ALF. What was her name?

HUGHIE. Jan. Jan Castle.

ALF. She's a funny girl, isn't she?

HUGHIE. Is she?

ALF. Yeah, she's a funny girl. I thought poor old Wacka'd wet himself. Do you really think she's the type for you to be goin' around with?

HUGHIE [*getting angry, holding on*]. What do you see as my type, Dad?

ALF. Well, she bungs it on a bit, don't she?

HUGHIE. Now listen——

ALF. Now you don't have to take offence, I haven't said nothin' but it just strikes me——

HUGHIE. What just strikes you?

ALF [*growing a little heated*]. You're only a kid, when you grow up a bit you'll see all her kind are the same. Got their money by keepin' the working man down and that's how they're gunna hang onto it.

HUGHIE. Oh, come off it.

ALF. Now, listen, my boy. I oughta know something. I know something about what goes on in the world. And I'm telling you, take it or leave it, I'm telling you, that young lady's too lah-dee-dah for us.

[48]

HUGHIE. Oh? What do you mean when you say US?

ALF. Our family. Us. [*A pause.*] Or don't you see eye to eye with us any more?

HUGHIE. I'm trying to work.

ALF. Yr mother spotted it first. You're gettin' big ideas—tryin' to move up in the world.

HUGHIE. Of course I am. Why shouldn't I?

ALF. Because we're working people, we've always been working people and working people we're gunna stay.

HUGHIE. I am doing what you want. Haven't you rammed it down my throat all my life, get an education, get out of the rut. Well, you can't do that without changing some way. If I'm changing it's through you, it's all through you.

ALF. That's not what I meant. A bit of study's all right to get you through exams, get you a good job, but all this standin' around spoutin' big ideas, going round with smart-arsed little sheilas from the North Shore—— [*He breaks, softens.*] It's all wrong, son. Can't you see?

HUGHIE. Look, I——

ALF. Yeah, I know something, I oughta know something. You'll see, son, you'll come round in time. Now you get on with your work.

HUGHIE. But——

ALF [*magnanimously*]. I don't want to argue with you. You know I can't stand fightin'. You just get into your study. You're right there, son. The study's the thing. [HUGHIE, *still furious, goes head down into his work again.*] Like me to clean yr shoes for tomorrow?

HUGHIE. Leave them, I'll do them.

[49]

ALF. I don't mind doin' 'em. Which ones are y'wearin'?

HUGHIE [*trying not to be irritable*]. Haven't thought.
These probably.

ALF. Well, give us 'em. [*He is on his knees, dragging shoes off.*]

HUGHIE. I said leave them.

ALF. No. No, let me. I c'n do yr shoes for you, can't I?
Gawd. [HUGHIE *shrugs, gives up the shoes.* ALF *takes them up to do them near sink bench.*] Hah! If anybody else asked me to clean their shoes for 'em . . .

HUGHIE. I don't like you doing that, Dad.

ALF. It's all right, it's all right, you get on with yr work.
[HUGHIE *does so but after a few seconds looks up and watches his father at work. Gradually he smiles.*

HUGHIE. Ay, Dad. Thanks for doing them.

ALF [*looks up, hesitates, grins*]. She's right.

CURTAIN

ACT TWO

SCENE ONE

Anzac Day. Behind the house the sky is dark. It is before dawn. A light is on in the kitchen. MUM, in her dressing gown, is getting a cup of tea. ALF, dressed in an old but neat blue suit, comes out of bedroom at rear, crosses lounge switching on light, and goes to door of HUGHIE's bedroom. He knocks gently on door. His manner when he calls to HUGHIE is unsure.

ALF. Err—er—wakey, wakey. Rise and shine. [*Louder*] Hughie! Er—Hughie! [*Listens.*] Come on, matey. 'Urry up.

> [ALF *hurries back across lounge, switches off light, switches it on again immediately and glares at a television set sitting in downstage corner facing up into room. Grunts, snaps light off again, goes into kitchen.*]

[*Grins at* DOT.] Got that cuppa tea ready, Mother?

MUM. No. I bin bakin' a cake. [*Hands him cup.*]

ALF [*taking it*]. Wouldn't be surprised what you did. Gawd, that kid can sleep. [*He sits, starts putting new lace into shoe.*] Why do your laces always snap when y'r runnin' late? They never go when y'got all day to fix it,

[51]

only when y'r runnin' late. [*Laughs.*] That's life, ay, Dot? [*He looks towards* HUGHIE'S *room, listens, the smile momentarily vanishing and a certain tension returning.*] [*Calls*] Ay, Hughie!

MUM. You make a fool of y'self over that boy.

ALF. Oh get out.

MUM. Y'give in to him. One minute you can't say enough about him, next thing you're all over him like a rash.

ALF [*smiles*]. Don't pick me, Mother. [*Sits, sugars tea.*] Not today. [*Grins happily.*] It's the old digger's day today.
[ALF *suddenly looks around restlessly.*
Knew there was someth'n wrong. No Wacka.

MUM [*nods*]. Mmm. Funny without Wack.

ALF [*a bit piqued*]. Never thought I'd see that you know. Wack not gettin' up to go to the Dawn Service. Not marchin' either.

MUM. Y'know 'is leg nearly went on 'im last year. It was me made him promise he wouldn't do no marchin' again. Standin' on his feet all that time with that leg.

ALF. You c'n be 'ard, Dot. Where's yr sentiment?

MUM. I face up to things. Not like you.

ALF. It's not the same without old Wack.

MUM. Lots of old blokes are droppin' out of it. Y'can't expect 'em to go on forever.

ALF. He's not that old. Lot of 'em older than him still march.

MUM. On a gammy leg? He'll be with y'in spirit, if that cheers you up. We'll be watchin'—in comfort.

[52]

ALF. Comfort. I dunno what this country's coming to. If I ever thought I'd see the day when people'd think of their own comfort on Anzac Day——

MUM. Well, I'm not sorry. It was Wacka's idea and it was a very nice thought hiring the television.

ALF. *Television.*

MUM. Don't you go 'im. If he gets 'ere before you go, don't you go 'im.

ALF. Television.

MUM. I noticed you looked at it last night.

ALF. Bloody cowboys and Indians. Bang, bang, bang—had a headache all night. I'll give 'im television.

MUM. You leave him alone. It was his idea and he's gunna enjoy it. [*Laughs.*] Best idea Wacka's had since we knew him.

ALF. Only one.

MUM. His landlady'll be wild he didn't put it in there.

ALF. I wouldn't care where he put it, he could shove it up his jumper for mine. [*Jumps up, drinks down last of tea.*] Well, while you two sit back like Lord and Lady Muck the two patriotic members of the family'll be there—in person. [*Yells*] Hughie!

[*The slightest pause.*

MUM [*softly*]. Hughie won't be goin' to no march.

ALF. Hughie's never missed a Dawn Service yet and he always come and watched me march after. What are y'talkin' about? Where's my medals? Hughie!

[*He marches across darkened lounge and raps on* HUGHIE'S *door.*

[53]

C'm'on, matey. Nearly dinnertime. We'll never get there. [*A pause.*] Hughie!

HUGHIE [*voice muffled, drowsy, from dark bedroom*]. What do you want?

ALF. Y'know the mob they get in Martin Place—if we don't get goin' we'll be stuck up the back. Come on, hurry it up.

HUGHIE. I'm not going.

ALF. Come on, son, we haven't got that much—— [*Then he registers.*] What did you say? [HUGHIE *doesn't answer.* ALF *suddenly rages*] What did you say?

> [ALF *throws the door open, switches on the light.* HUGHIE, *in pyjamas, rolls over, props himself up on one elbow. They look at each other in silence.*

HUGHIE. I'm not going.

ALF. You get up out of that bed or I'll——

HUGHIE. I'm tired.

> [*He reaches up, switches off light switch near bed. Out of the dark comes* ALF'S *roar of rage. He flings out of the room, slamming the door. And charges across the lounge into the bedroom at rear.*
> [MUM *has heard it all from kitchen, now goes into lounge. She is about to switch on light when* ALF *comes charging out of bedroom. He is viciously jabbing his long-service medals into his coat and almost collides with her in centre of room. She grabs him by shoulders, steadies him. They stand still facing each other.*
> [*Light spills across the room from open door of kitchen and their bedroom.*

[54]

MUM. Alf——

ALF. Who does 'e think he is?

MUM. Gimme those. [*She takes medals from him and pins them carefully.*] You want them to look right, don't you?

ALF. What's the matter with the lot of yz? What's come-overyer?

MUM. Now . . .

ALF. Well . . . Gawd . . .

MUM. Don't get y'self worked up, love.

ALF. Well, you know what day this is. This day used to mean someth'n' once. [*She opens her mouth to speak.*] Don't shut me up, I'm not ashamed of it. I'm proud to be a bloody Australian. If it wasn't for men like my old man this country'd never bin heard of. They put Australia on the map they did, the Anzacs did. An' bloody died doin' it. Well, even a snotty-nosed little kid oughta be proud of that. What's happened to him? Why isn't he?

MUM. Don't you go using this as an excuse for one of your——

ALF [*quietly*]. One of my what?

MUM. You know what.

ALF. I don't need no excuse today. It's my day, see.

MUM [*as he moves towards door*]. What time'll y'be home?

ALF. When I get here.

MUM. Alf——

ALF. You know I never know what time I'll get home on Anzac Day.

MUM. And what d'you think you're gunna get up to?

[55]

ALF. I'm gunna celebrate this day the way I always cele-
brated this day. That's all. [*He shoots one glance towards*
HUGHIE'S *room.*] Little *runt*.

> [*He goes out quickly.*
> [*A pause.* MUM *walks back to kitchen, switches off
> light. Stands thoughtfully in lounge. Crosses, stands
> outside* HUGHIE'S *room.*

MUM [*quietly*] Hughie. [*A pause.*] You're not asleep.

HUGHIE [*quietly*]. What do you want?

MUM [*after a pause*]. Do you want me to get you a cup of
tea?

HUGHIE [*softening a little*]. No thanks, Mum.

MUM. All right. [*She is about to move away.*]

HUGHIE. I thought you were going to go off at me.

MUM. Hughie, what's the good in goin' off at you? [*Slight
break before she manages to say it.*] Y'don't see things the
same as us any more and that's that. I knew you wouldn't
go with him. Y'might've give 'im a bit of warning, that's
all.

HUGHIE. I'm sorry. How did you know?

MUM. I didn't come down in the last shower.

HUGHIE. Why didn't you tell him then, Mum? You could
have softened the blow.

MUM. You fight your own battles. I'm not buyin' into any
arguments. I get enough of 'em around here.

HUGHIE. Mum . . . [*He stops.*]

MUM. What?

HUGHIE. Nothing.

[56]

MUM. Go to sleep. I'm going back to bed. [*She goes towards bedroom.*] Wacka can let himself in.

[*She goes into bedroom, shuts door. Its light goes out. General lighting fades momentarily to suggest a passing of time.*

[*Light fades in again, held down very softly. The sky behind the house has traces of pink through it. Very gradually it begins to lighten.*

[*In* HUGHIE'S *bedroom some slight movement. He lights a cigarette, lies back, hand behind head. Then he flicks radio on. Its small light glows softly in dark.*

[*Steps are heard approaching. The front door opens,* WACKA *is silhouetted against light from sky spilling through door. He comes in, leaving door open to give himself some light. Crosses to lounge windows, quietly pulls up blinds. Dawn light comes in. He looks around, moves quietly back to door.*

[*He is about to close it but a sudden quickening of light all through the sky stops him. He takes a step outside, looks up at the sky. It is dawn. He stands very still as though listening for something.*

[WACKA *turns, comes back to door. Stands another second or two then shrugs, laughs quietly to himself. But still he stands, looking out and up. There is absolute silence.*

WACKA [*to himself, so quietly it can hardly be heard*]. It was now. [*He stands still, remembering.*]

[*And out of the silence comes, soft and distant, the sound of a trumpet playing "The Last Post".*

[WACKA *stands as though paralysed. As it plays through, the bedroom door opens and* MUM *stands*

[57]

there without putting on the light. She is fussily wrapping gown about her but the sound stops her. She sees WACKA'S *face, the dawn gradually lighting it, and she does not move. They both stand listening. The last notes die away.*

[*For a moment neither one moves.*

[*Shakes his head, comes back to earth.*] Where'd that come from?

MUM. Hughie's room, I think. [HUGHIE *switches the radio off.*] He must've put the wiless on to hear the service.

WACKA. Didn't 'e go?

[MUM *shakes her head, stares across towards his room, her usually set expression about to break into a grudging smile.*

MUM. Funny kid. [*Snaps out of it.*] Waste of time tryin' to sleep. May as well stay up now. I'll get you a cuppa tea.

[*They go towards kitchen.*

[*Lights fade.*

SCENE TWO

A few hours later. Daylight.

WACKA *sits in lounge room, his chair pulled out near centre of room, watching TV. Noise is heard from the set . . . marching feet, a band playing in the distance, a commentator's voice. Light from the television set plays up into the room and over* WACKA'S *face. The front door is shut and some of the window blinds down. One blind is up and lets some daylight into the room.* WACKA *watches*

[58]

in a kind of stupefied delight, wriggling in his chair, grin-
ning, a look of half-disbelief on his face.

WACKA [*yelling*]. Ay, Dot. Come'n 'ave a look. Ay,
Hughie.

> [HUGHIE *comes out of his room. He wears sports*
> *slacks and thong sandals, is in T-shirt and carries*
> *coloured sports shirt and shoes.*

Look at it. Look at it.

> [*Over his shoulder* WACKA *sees that* HUGHIE *is occupied*
> *with his shoes and socks.*

Come on, Hughie.

HUGHIE [*irritably*]. I don't WANT to look at it.

> [*Then is immediately sorry.*

March still going?

> [WACKA *nods without taking his eyes from it.*

HUGHIE [*unable to resist a glance or two at it*]. See anybody
you know?

WACKA. Oh don't be mad. Y'wouldn't see anyone.

HUGHIE. Why not. They get in very close.

WACKA. Y'see it better than bein' there. I reckon you do.
Y'see it better than bein' there.

> [MUM *comes out of bedroom, in old floppy frock,*
> *loose cardigan and slippers.*

Come'n look at this, Dot.

MUM. I've got to get into these dishes.

HUGHIE. Leave 'em.

MUM [*she joins him as he says above*]. Leave 'em. I know.
You and yr father.

[59]

HUGHIE. It's a holiday, isn't it? Why don't you sit down?

MUM. Where?

HUGHIE [*making room for her on the lounge*]. Sorry.

MUM. I want to sit closer than that, I'll never see it.

HUGHIE. If we *must* look at it, this is the right distance. [*But despite himself he still keeps glancing at it.*] You're supposed to sit back from it.

WACKA. You was sittin' too close last night. Ruins yr eyes.

MUM. Ay? Oh well, all right. [*She goes to lounge, collapses in it. Sinking back into its deepest hollow and spreading herself.*] I didn't put me stays on. Not going out.

WACKA. Y'don't wanna get all dolled up. Relax 'n' look at this.

[MUM *watches it awhile.*

MUM. It's different to what I thought.

HUGHIE [*still playing truculent*]. Why?

MUM. I thought it'd be all blurred. Where's that from? They're up high there——

HUGHIE. Bebarfalds' corner. Camera must be on the awning. Catches each lot as they come round the corner.

MUM. It's real clear, look at their medals.

WACKA. It's good, isn't it?

MUM. Look, it's rainin'. You c'n see it comin' down. Ttt! Ever know an Anzac Day it didn't rain?

WACKA. Dozens of 'em.

MUM. Always seems to be rainin' to me. [*To* HUGHIE] You goin' out?

HUGHIE. I told you at breakfast time——

[60]

WACKA [*suddenly almost screaming, recoiling in his chair*].
Look! *Look!*

MUM. What the hell's the——?

WACKA. Fred! Freddie Watson! 'E's comin' right into
it . . . look! . . . 'E's gone. [*He sits again, mouth open,
turns to* MUM, *who is laughing at him.*] I never thought . . .
[*Shakes his head.*] Well. [*Can't stop shaking it.*] Well.

MUM. Keep lookin'. Y'might see Alf.

WACKA [*after staring at her open-mouthed as he registers
this new thought*]. No. No, our mob ain't come down.

[*A car's brakes squeal outside. Horn starts honking.*

MUM [*looking over her shoulder*]. Make a noise, why
dontcher?

[HUGHIE *jumps up, looks out of window.*

HUGHIE. It's Jan.

MUM [*startled*]. Ay?

HUGHIE [*tucking shirt in*]. Jan. I told you I was going out
with her.

MUM. You didn't say nothin' about her comin' here.

WACKA [*eyes on set*]. Ssh, ssh.

[HUGHIE *has hurried to door, opens it, waves.*

HUGHIE. Hi.

MUM [*sitting up*]. She's not comin' in? [*In panic, struggling
to get up from lounge.*] You little *bugger*. Why didn't
y'tell me, I could've put on something decent. [*Grabs
her spare tyre.*] Oh! Oh, Hughie!

HUGHIE. She won't look at you. [*Yells out of door*] Come
on!

WACKA [*registering for first time*]. What's the matter?

[61]

MUM. It's her.

HUGHIE [*turning quickly to her*]. You said she could come again.

[JAN *hurries in.*

JAN. Couldn't find my cigarettes. [*Coming down to* MUM] Mrs. Cook—no, stay there, don't get up. Oh, Mr.— Mr.——

HUGHIE. Dawson.

JAN. Dawson. This must be a thrill for you.

[WACKA *is hit with shyness again, nods, grins, looks wildly at* MUM *then back at set.*

HUGHIE. Where do you want to sit?

JAN. Anywhere. [*She and* HUGHIE *perch up on arms of chair behind and higher than the others, looking down on the proceedings. They are close to each other.*] Good picture.

HUGHIE. No outside aerial either.

JAN [*takes one long look at picture on screen.*] My God. Will you look at them? What *do* they look like?

[*A pause.* WACKA *and* HUGHIE *look at screen, commentator's voice drones on.* MUM'S *head slowly turns around and she looks up at* JAN.

MUM. Well? What *do* they look like?

JAN. Oh, I wish Australian men would learn how to dress——

MUM [*she thinks about this, then*]. What's dress got to do with it?

HUGHIE. You've got to admit, Mum, they are conservative. Look at all those double-breasted suits——

[62]

MUM. Your Dad's got 'is double-breaster on same as all of them. What d'you think 'e'd wear? Overalls?

JAN. 'Ray! Single-breasted suit. Nice stripe too.

HUGHIE. Off the hook.

JAN. Oh, of course, but quite smart. There's another. Younger chaps, of course.

MUM. You seem to know a lòt about men's fashions.

JAN. Mmm? Don't know anything about them but, naturally, we're all interested in clothes——

[MUM *nods, lips pursed, looks back at set.*

HUGHIE [*half-smiling*]. They don't look real bad, you know.

[JAN *looks up at him, surprised.*

JAN. Hughie!

HUGHIE. Look at them. Serious as anything. They're sort of proud but not——

JAN. Not what?

HUGHIE. I don't know. Not military. Not aggressive. You know?

JAN. Hughie, really.

WACKA [*suddenly*]. Ssh!! [*He is pointing, almost paralysed with excitement.*] Ssh!

MUM. What? What is it? [*Looks at set. Flatly*] There's Alf.

WACKA. Look at him, look at him—he's up the back, he's comin' close now. [*On his feet.*] Look at him! Look! He's comin' straight towards us.

JAN. Who is it?

[63]

HUGHIE. Dad. [*He stands up, oddly excited.*]

[WACKA *is crouched in front of set.*

MUM. What's he got his chest stuck out like that for, silly old cow?

WACKA. Gee, he looks good. He looks real good.

MUM. His suit looks awful. I don't know, I pressed it.

WACKA. Get the walk, will ya? Get the walk on it!

MUM. Cocky? Look at him!

> [*And suddenly they all burst into laughter. Just as suddenly* HUGHIE'S *laughter stops. He looks at picture, a battle of feelings inside him, and chokes up.* MUM *and* WACKA *don't see.* JAN, *still laughing, looks up at* HUGHIE *as he turns away quickly.*

MUM. He's gone. [*She sits back.*]

JAN. What is the matter, Hughie?

HUGHIE. Right as rain. [*Covers up quickly.*] Gee, he looked an old idiot, didn't he?

MUM [*who has been laughing to herself, stops*]. No, he didn't.

HUGHIE [*recovering*]. Well, you were laughing.

MUM. It was just the shock, seeing him, plain as day. I wasn't laughing *at* 'im.

HUGHIE. Well, I was! [*But the feelings are still mixed.*] He looked such a big aleck, marching along as though he'd won both wars single-handed. It was—pathetic.

JAN. Oh, they all are.

MUM [*huffily*]. Turn it off, Wack.

WACKA. Ay?

MUM. Haven't y'seen enough?

[64]

WACKA [looks from her to JAN, gets up reluctantly, goes to set]. Oh. Yeah, yes, Dot. It's all the same. [He switches it off.] Good seein' yr mates, but.

MUM. It was very nice. Pity more people don't appreciate it.

WACKA. Oh, they still get a good rollup. Well . . . [He stands about uncomfortably.]

JAN. Are we going?

HUGHIE. Suppose so. Do we still want to do this?

JAN. I want to do it very much. Don't you?

HUGHIE [slight hesitation. Nods]. It's just not as easy for me as I'd thought. I'll get the camera. [Moves away, turns suddenly to face her. She has turned to watch MUM and WACKA. He turns and goes to his room.)

> [A silence. MUM sits drumming her fingers on arm of couch. WACKA goes up to windows, pulls up blinds. He begins to whistle softly "Take me back to dear old Blighty". JAN watches him, smiles, relaxes.

JAN. Mr. Dawson seems bright today.

MUM [indignantly]. He is not. He 'asn't 'ad a drink.

JAN. That's what I mean. The other night he had had a drink and he seemed very quiet.

MUM. No one gets a look-in when Hughie's Dad's around.

JAN. Mrs. Cook . . . Hughie thought I was rude the other night. I was too. I'm sorry.

MUM [embarrassed]. Hughie's dopey. It was all right. [WACKA comes down.] Hughie's friend reckons she likes you better sober.

[65]

JAN [*laughs*]. I didn't say that, really. But this is your day, isn't it?

MUM. Oh, don't start him on that, get enougha that from Alf.

JAN. But isn't it? You *were* there. Do you still remember it, Mr. Dawson?

WACKA [*nods shyly*]. Yeah.

JAN [*prompting him*]. What do you remember?

WACKA. Not much. It was a long while ago. [*Silence again.*]

JAN. Were you at the actual first landing? On this very day?

WACKA [*nods*]. Yeah. Thought about it this morn'n'. Before sunup. Just about the time we started up them rocks.

MUM. What was y'thinkin' then, love?

WACKA. 'Ow do I know, it was years ago.

MUM. No, I mean th's morn'n'.

WACKA. Oh. [*To* JAN] I was standin' in that door lookin' at the sky, I was miles away, dreamin' about it. And I 'eard the Last Post. Dinkum, I thought they was comin' for me.

MUM. Hughie had the service on on 'is wiless.

JAN. Hughie did? I thought he hated Anzac Day.

MUM. Hughie? Hughie hate——? Why should he?

JAN. Well, all it stands for. [*She looks at them as though they will understand. They don't.*]

MUM. Such as what?

JAN. The same old cliches in the newspapers year after year. All the public hoo-ha—it's so damned——

[66]

[MUM *and* WACKA *exchange a look. She sees they are not with her, struggles to explain.*

I mean—I'm sorry—but—to us, to the people coming on, there's something quite—offensive in the way you all cling to it. Not Mr. Dawson, it really happened to him, he knows what he feels today and why, it's not just because it's expected. But with so many people it's——

MUM. It's what?

JAN [*shrugging*]. Well, isn't it all rather phoney?

[HUGHIE *is back.*

HUGHIE. Right? [*No one speaks. He looks around.*] What's up?

MUM. It's on again. [*She looks at* JAN *with the old disapproval.*]

[HUGHIE *crosses quickly, gets* JAN *to her feet.*

HUGHIE. Best we get going.

WACKA [*looking at the camera*]. Going for a picnic?

HUGHIE. What? No. [*Grimly*] A little job. A job I've been promising myself I'd do for years. [*To* JAN] But I'd feel happier if you weren't so—— [*He stops.*] Come on.

[*They start to go out.*

MUM [*calling after them*]. What time'll you be home?

HUGHIE. Expect me when you see me. Don't save tea.

JAN. 'Bye.

MUM. I wish someone in this house'd tell me occasionally where they're goin' and when they'll be back.

WACKA. What's the job? What was he talkin' about?

MUM. I don't know. What was *she* talkin' about?

[67]

WACKA [*shakes his head*]. Didn't foller it. Didn't get a word. Never do when she starts.

MUM. Hughie's the same when he gets goin'.

WACKA. Gawd, we must be gettin' old, Dot.

MUM [*grimly*]. Either we're old—or they're terrible young.

All right, we're old — but, by Gad,

[*Lights fade.*

SCENE THREE

Anzac Day. Evening. MUM *is in kitchen, washing dishes at the sink, from a meal she and* WACKA *evidently shared. The rest of the house is in darkness.* WACKA *comes in through back door of kitchen. He has had a couple of drinks, is not, however, even remotely drunk, just a little loosened up. He carries a bottle wrapped in newspaper.*

WACKA. There, wasn't long.

MUM. Y'ave a drink?

WACKA. Coupla short snorts. [*He has put bottle down on table. Starts to get glasses to pour them a drink.*] Y'oughta see the mob in the wine bar. Real old blokes—and all the old girls.

MUM. I wouldn't be seen dead in those places. What did you get?

WACKA Bottla muscat. All right?

MUM. It's too sweet, that stuff. I won't have any.

WACKA. Go on, be in it.

MUM. May as well. Right. [*The latter as she finishes drying dishes and puts tea towel up. Comes to table, sits.*] What's the time, Wack?

[68]

WACKA. Seven o'clock nearly. [*Looks at her quickly.*] He oughta be home soon now the pubs are shut.

MUM. I'm not worried about Alf. I'd like to know what that young Hughie's up to.

WACKA. Now. Give 'im a go with 'is girl. [*Drinks.*] Beats me, that girl. She's got Gallipoli on the brain.

MUM. Same as Alf. [*Then with a laugh*] Wouldn't he be wild if he heard that? Him and her the same. [*Drinks.*] It's not Gallipoli with him, it's Anzac Day. This time o'year I get sick of the sound of it.

WACKA. He'll be right tonight when he gets home.

MUM. I hope he's had too much to drink.

WACKA. Ay?

MUM. I hope he's had too much. If he's had too much he's just sick, he falls straight into bed. If he hasn't had enough to make him sick he just gets steamed up and we'll cop the lot. Australia for the Australians.

WACKA [*smiles*]. Poor old Alf.

[*She looks at him suddenly and is serious.*

MUM. Well, that's a turnup. Him, he's always Poor old Wack and how y'need lookin' after.

WACKA. Oh, I let him say it.

MUM. Yeah, y'gotta nurse 'im a bit. [*Quietly*] I don't begrudge him his few drinks with his old mates. Let him enjoy it, he doesn't play up much. [WACKA *laughs quietly, thinking about* ALF.] [*She looks at him.*] You've had a quiet old Anzac Day, haven't you?

WACKA [*shrugs*]. Oh . . .

MUM. Tell y'someth'n'. That upset Alf a bit before he even got goin' th's morn'n'. No Wacka.

[69]

WACKA. I didn't get on it with him last year, year before either, come to that.

MUM. No, but it was the Service, not goin' to the Service.

WACKA. Oh I'm gettin' too old to care about all that, Dot. [*A bit sheepishly*] That's terrible, accordin' to Alf, but——

MUM. You do as you please, don't let him bluff you. I d'know why he still sticks to it.

WACKA [*thinks about it; quietly*]. Alf still hankers after things. I'm older, Dot. I don't hanker any more.

MUM. I wonder what he thinks about. Lotta nights he can't sleep, y'know. Lies there thinkin'. [*They have become very quiet, speak in a desultory fashion almost to themselves.*] He always wanted to be an engineer, y'know.

WACKA. I know. He told me often enough.

MUM. 'E should've gone into the Engineers during the war, that worried him all the war. He told me after.

WACKA. I know, I was there. [*Chuckles.*] The bloody Poms was runnin' the whole show and stoppin' 'im goin' where he wanted, accordin' to Alf.

MUM. They wouldn't take him without any qualifications, couldn't expect 'em to. HE expected 'em to. Well, what qualifications would he have had? Done no trainin', went through the Depression pickin' up someth'n' here, someth'n' there, workin' on the roads, anyth'n'. He never even got started in engineering.

WACKA [*bottle over her glass*]. Want another one?

MUM. Just a little one, may as well be silly as the way we are.

WACKA. All the best.

[70]

MUM. All the best. [*They drink.*] Poor old Alf. I s'pose he hasn't had much of a go. [*She flashes a glance at* WACKA *who is smiling sympathetically into his plonk.*] Neither've you for that matter.

WACKA. Me? [*He is a little surprised.*] I been right, Dot, I always been right.

MUM. Go on. You was hurt worse than him, bin on the pension.

WACKA. I'm right.

> [MUM *looks at him for some moments. He is rolling a cigarette and doesn't notice in her gaze there is a long-held rarely-expressed affection.*

MUM. Y'know someth'n'? All the talk Alf does about the Anzacs, I don't reckon I've heard you say more than five words about it all these years.

WACKA [*laughs*]. When Alf's around I leave the talkin' to Alf.

MUM. Now today when she was here—that's the first time I've heard you mention Gallipoli in years. Not that you said that much.

WACKA. I wouldn't tell her.

MUM. I think she was dinkum. She just wanted to know about what it was like bein' there. [*A pause.*] What was it like, Wack?

WACKA [*he doesn't answer right away, thinks about it, immediately becomes self-conscious*]. Oh, I d'know.

MUM. Go on. Tell us.

WACKA. Nothin' to tell. It was just—— Oh, I d'know. [*But he is dreaming away about it as he speaks.*]

[71]

MUM. Y'can't say y'dunno. You was at it, you seen the whole thing.

WACKA. No, I didn't. Nobody did. Want another one?

MUM. Haven't finished this. You can taste the grape in it all right.

WACKA [*pours his slowly. Sits thinking, continues quietly, almost to himself*]. Nobody seen the whole thing that day. All you seen was what y'was doin' y'self. And then y'couldn't hardly see more than a few feet ahead of yer.

MUM. Why, love?

WACKA [*reluctantly*]. Well . . . [*feels for the words*] it was the terrain. [*He thinks about it, continues, gradually warming up*] Y'never seen such hills in y'r life. They musta thought we was bloody mountain goats to send us up'm. [*Pause. She waits. He continues quietly*] When we landed on the beach it was still dark. The current'd carried us down a bit far, everything was disorganised. Well—we had to get up them hills just the same. Y'didn't know where the old Turk was or how many of'm was up top, but y'knew they was sittin' up there like Jackie waitin' to pick y'all off as y'climbed.

MUM. Was you scared?

WACKA [*nods*]. Yeah.

MUM [*with rather automatic sympathy*]. Must've bin terrible.

WACKA. It was the feelin' of not gettin' anywhere, that was the worst. [*He is hardly conscious of her now: stares straight ahead: goes over it all virtually to himself.*] [*Jerks his attention back to her again.*] It was all declivities, see. Declivities. 'Oles and slopes and dirty big boulders. And bare.

Bare. I never seen country like it before or since, even out here.

MUM. But where was the fightin', the battle, like?

WACKA. All round yer. Noise, crikey. Y'd never know who'd come over the next rise at yer, burst of gunfire or bloody Turk. [*He slows: then gravely*] Then when the sun come up y'could see yr mates . . . bodies . . . corpses everywhere . . . blood and everything . . . [*A pause.*] Sometimes y'd be runnin' and y'd hear a noise and it'd be y'self sorta screamin'. Y'd have yr bayonet out and when they came at y' . . . [*He stops.*] Y'couldn't stop 'n' help yr mates, that was the worst . . . y'had to keep pushin' on.

MUM. What happened in the end?

WACKA. We got together again, some'ow. Some of us. Soon we was all dug in, up and down them hills. We stayed there in the stinkin' heat with the stinkin' flies 'n' the bully beef 'n' dysentery and sometimes the Turk trenches not ten yards away—we stayed there nine months. Then we pulled out, whole bang lot of us. [*He pauses. Laughs softly.*] When we went in there we was nobody. When we come out we was famous. [*Smiles.*] Anzacs. [*Shakes his head.*] Ballyhoo. Photos in the papers. Famous. Not worth a crumpet. [*Drinks.*] Sorry, Dot. Didn't mean t'bash yr ear. Gett'n' like Alf.

MUM. Except you've got someth'n' to talk about. 'E's all wind. [*Studies him a moment.*] Well, I d'know. Y'bin through the lot. Two wars 'n' a depression. Y'got no family, a room in a boardin' 'ouse—and us. And that's the issue. Now, if Alf was you he'd have a reason to be crooked on the world. But—y'never say a word.

[73]

WACKA [*reflects: smiles*]. Well, I'm all right. I've settled for what I've got.

> [*The front door opens, light goes on in the lounge. It is* HUGHIE, *home again and full of excitement.*

MUM. That you, Alf?

HUGHIE. Me. [*Goes to his room, puts on light, is singing "77 Sunset Strip" or "Surfside Six" or some such. Holds camera tight and up to his face.*] Oh, you beauty. You little beauty. [*He kisses camera, puts it tenderly on top of cabinet.*]

MUM. Have you had any tea?

HUGHIE [*calls*]. We had a hamburger at the Cross.

MUM. What was y'doin' up there?

> [HUGHIE *is whipping shoes off, getting into his thongs. At her question he looks up impatiently.*

HUGHIE. I just told you. Having a hamburger.

MUM [*to* WACKA]. I d'know what we're sittin' in here for. Come inside.

> [WACKA *and* MUM *rise,* WACKA *taking his glass and bottle. They go into lounge.*

WACKA. Don't y'want another drink?

MUM. No, I've had enough of that stuff.

WACKA. Will we put the television on?

MUM [*impatiently*]. In a minute. Hughie!

> [HUGHIE *is lying flat on his back on the bed.*

HUGHIE. What do you want?

MUM. You gettin' changed?

HUGHIE. No.

[74]

MUM. What are y'doin' in there?

HUGHIE. Smoking a reefer.

MUM. What?

HUGHIE. Having a drag. Marijuana. Feelthy pictures on the ceiling.

MUM [*to* WACKA]. What'd he say? [*To* HUGHIE] You wouldn't say Hullo when you come in, would you?

HUGHIE. Hullo.

MUM [*sharply*]. Hughie . . .

HUGHIE. Oh, all right. [*He rises, gets pullover, comes out putting it on.*]

MUM [*before he gets there*]. I'm gunna have a go at that boy before he's finished. Haven't said a word to 'im for weeks, he's gone his own way but I'm gunna have a go at 'im.

WACKA [*looks at his muscat bottle, grins*]. It's a good brand all right.

> [HUGHIE *has joined them. He stands looking a little defiantly at his mother, then relents.*

HUGHIE. Hullo.

MUM. What y'bin doing all day?

HUGHIE. Had a ball! [*Going to lounge, flops into it.*] Oh, the pictures I got! You oughta see the pictures I got.

MUM. What pictures?

HUGHIE. For our story. I told you—for the Uni paper, story on Anzac Day. Jan's writing it.

MUM. You started late enough, it was all over practically before you even left.

HUGHIE. WHAT was all over?

[75]

MUM. The march and everything.

HUGHIE. I wasn't after the march. You'll see half a page of all that crap in the Tele tomorrow. Oh, golly, and to think I nearly didn't want to go. Came to my senses all right once I saw it again.

[*Slight pause.* MUM *and* WACKA *exchange a glance.*

WACKA [*tentatively*]. What sort of pictures did you take, son?

HUGHIE [*sitting up; faces them seriously*]. Anzac Day. As it is. I got some beauties.

MUM. How do you know if they're any good?

HUGHIE. When we finished this arvo we shot in to a mate of mine, runs a photography place in town, and we could see right away.

MUM [*irritably*]. But what was they pictures *of*?

HUGHIE. Everything. [*Sarcastically*] The celebration. There's one, one terrific one—pure fluke how I got it— of an old man lying flat on his back in a lane near a pub. Boy, had he had it?

[WACKA *starts to laugh, picturing it.* MUM *silences him with a look.*

MUM. What'd y'want to take a picture of that for?

HUGHIE. That's the point of it. They're all like that. Outside a pub near Central there was a character sitting on the footpath leaning up against a post. He had the most terrific face, hadn't shaved, few teeth missing, very photogenic. I snuck up near him and squatted down and . . . oh, just as I got it framed up, it was wonderful. He vomited. Just quietly. All down his chin, all down the front of his coat. I took it.

[76]

[WACKA *has been about to drink from his glass of wine, lowers it and pushes it away from him.*

MUM [*evenly*]. You're goin' to put that in a paper?

HUGHIE. Are we ever?

MUM [*after a blank pause*]. Why?

HUGHIE. Because we're sick of all the muck that's talked about this day . . . the great national day of honour, day of memory, day of salute to the fallen, day of grief . . . It's just one long grog-up.

MUM. But——

HUGHIE. No buts. I know what you lot think about it, everyone your age is the same. Well, I've seen enough Anzac Days to know what *I* think of them. And that's what I got today in my little camera. What I think of it.

MUM. You can't put that sort of thing in a paper.

HUGHIE. Just watch us.

MUM. It's more than that. Anzac Day's more than that.

HUGHIE. Yeah, it's a lot of old hasbeens getting up in the local RSL and saying, Well, boys, you all know what we're here for, we're here to honour our mates who didn't come back. And they all feel sad and have another six or seven beers.

MUM. Hughie——

HUGHIE. Look, no argument. You think what you like, I've had to put up with that all my life, well now you can just put up with my views. If they don't agree, bad luck.

MUM. Y'd better not let yr father hear y'talkin' like this. 'E'd better not know nothin' about this thing goin' in the paper.

[77]

HUGHIE. He's got to know sooner or later.

MUM. Yr gettin' carried away. Just because a coupla blokes get a few in——

HUGHIE. Couple? Everywhere you look—every suburb you go through—and we went through them today—every pub, every street—all over this damned country today men got rotten. This is THE day. [*In a dinkum-Aussie speech-maker's voice*] "When Awstrylia first reached maturity as a nation." [*His own voice*] Maturity! God!

WACKA [*shyly*]. 'Scuse me, lad.

HUGHIE. What?

WACKA. That's not all it is.

HUGHIE. Oh, Wacka.

WACKA [*gently*]. Can't you let 'em enjoy it? You don't have to agree. But they've got a right to their feelings.

HUGHIE. Wacka—you've been brought up on the speeches. They say what it's officially supposed to be. I've been looking at what it is. As far as I'm concerned, that's all it is. A great big meaningless booze-up. Nothing more.

MUM [*snapping*]. Well, y'r wrong.

[*From outside a crash. Then* ALF'S *voice in a burst of drunken profanity.*

HUGHIE [*gently*]. Am I?

[*Another crash. A burst of bawdy song.*

MUM. Alf.

WACKA [*listening*]. 'E 'ad too much?

[ALF *roars again.*

MUM. No. Not enough. [*To* HUGHIE] Now you be careful what you say.

[78]

[The door flies open. ALF *totters in. He is dishevelled. Hair flies wild, face is heavy with grog, trousers hang below his waist, shirt hangs half out. Clothes are sodden with spilled grog. He carries bottles, wrapped and unwrapped, and lurches to table, starting his dissertation as soon as he gets in.*

ALF. 'Ullo!! You buggers on the plonk? *[Wags finger at* MUM.] Y'know what it says on the wileless, when yr drinkin' don't drive when yr drivin' don't drink, Christ, 've I 'ad a day? I've had a bloody lovely day. I seen everybody, Dot—Wack—Wack—I seen everybody, what y'doin', 'Ughie, siddown yr makin' me giddy, I seen everybody. Old Bert Charles, y'oughter see old Bert Charles, he's eighteen stone an' pisspot, c'n 'e drink? Oh, Jeez, we started at a pub in King Street straight after the march, I was with Bluey Norton an' Ginger Simms, did we get on it? We bin there 'about an hour in comes ole Fred Harvey, I sung out You old bastard and 'e come up t'me y'know wot 'e did, 'e put on a voice like a bloody panz and 'e sez up high like, "Darl, 'ow ARE yer?" An' 'e kisses me, right in the bloody public bar, front of everyone, laugh, thought we'd bloody die, I hit him one and then we all 'ad a couple of grogs and then Ginge said I gotta meet me ole mate down the Quay, come'n meet me ole mate down the Quay, so we goes, whole lot of us goes and all the way down Fred does this act makin' up to the other blokes, laugh, I never laughed so much, on the way we picks up Johnny 'Opkins with 'is gammy leg—— *[A foggy glare towards* WACKA.] *He* marched, he was in the march—and 'e was sittin' in the gutter lookin' for the lav so we got 'im to 'is feet and shot 'im into a public lav and

[79]

in the lav there was a brawl, broken bottles flyin' everywhere and blood, Gawd, blood, and off we all went to Plasto's and there's Ginge's mates, we was there hours, hours, then we says let's get out'f 'ere and we're off up Pitt Street, we went into every pub, every pub we come to, we went in every pub, there was ten of us by then, ten of us so someone says Come on let's get some other bastards 'n' make it a round dozen, so we grabs two ole blokes and turned out they was real old diggers, real Anzacs, 'ear that Wack, Anzacs, they was sittin' 'avin' a quiet yarn to themselves, we soon fixed that—we got 'em and shouted 'em and Ginge 'e made a speech, 'e said these are the blokes wot started the Anzac legend, these done the trick, soldiers and bloody gentlemen and we poured bloody beer into the poor old cows till they couldn't stand up, they was rotten, then silly bloody Johnny 'Opkins 'as to go 'n' muck things, 'e turns round too quick and gets all dizzy and spews, did 'e spew, brought it all up all over the bloody bar, all over the mob, in their beer, all over the floor, all over 'mself, laugh . . . Jeez, I never laughed so much in all me . . .

[*Very early on* HUGHIE *has turned to face his mother and* WACKA. *As* ALF *drives remorselessly on* HUGHIE *watches their faces gradually change.* MUM, *who had been laughing at first, looks at* HUGHIE *long and steadily then slowly sits.* WACKA *looks completely embarrassed, not at first but very gradually, finally drops his glance, can't face* HUGHIE, *makes feeble attempt to quieten* ALF, *then stands looking down uncomfortably.*

[80]

[ALF *has at last realised something is wrong. His voice dies away. He turns, looks groggily at them all.*

ALF. What's the matter? What's up?

[*Nobody speaks.*

HUGHIE. You've just proved something.

ALF. What? [*Sways, tries to focus.*] What'd I prove?

MUM. Y'didn't prove nothin'. [*To* HUGHIE] You leave him alone, Hughie.

HUGHIE. Nothing to say. It's all been said. [*He starts to go.*]

ALF [*blearily*]. What'd 'e say? What'd 'e say?

HUGHIE. Forget it. You had a great day, that's all that matters.

ALF [*suddenly swinging* HUGHIE *around*]. You bein' funny? You playin' up again, Mr. Bloody Brains Trust?

HUGHIE [*quietly*]. Why couldn't you leave them alone? Those two poor old boys having their quiet talk? Does everyone have to be as rotten as you are before you can enjoy Anzac Day?

ALF [*very quietly*]. Watch y'self. Watch y'self, mister. [*To* MUM] Is that what he's on now? 'E's pickin' on the old diggers now?

HUGHIE [*breaking away in sudden burst of complete exasperation*]. Oh, frig the old diggers.

ALF [*weaving after him unsteadily*]. Why—you . . . you . . .

HUGHIE [*swinging on him*]. Do you know what you're celebrating today? [*To* MUM] Do *you*? Do you even know what it all meant? Have you ever bothered to dig a bit, find out what really happened back there, what this day meant?

[81]

MUM. I bin talkin' to Wacka about it just tonight——–

HUGHIE. Oh, Wacka––what would he know about it?

ALF. Don't you insult my mate, don't you insult him. He was there, wasn't he?

HUGHIE. What does the man who was there ever know about anything? All he knows is what he saw, one man's view from a trench. It's the people who come after, who can study it all, see the whole thing for what it was——

ALF [*with deepest contempt*]. Book-learnin'. [*Points to* WACKA.] He bloody suffered, that man. You tell me book-learnin' after the event's gunna tell y'more about it than he knows?

HUGHIE. Wacka was an ordinary soldier who did what he was told. He and his mates became a legend, all right, they've had to live up to it. Every year on the great day they've had to do the right thing, make the right speeches, talk of the dead they left there. But did any of them ever sit down and look back at that damn stupid climb up those rocks to see what it meant?

ALF. How do you know so much?

HUGHIE. How do I *know*? Didn't you shove it down my throat? [*He has plunged over to bookcase against wall, drags out large book.*] It's here. Encyclopaedia for Australian kids. You gave it to me yourself. Used to make me read the Anzac chapter every year. Well, I read it. The official history, all very glowing and patriotic. I read it . . . enough times to start seeing through it. [*He has been leafing through book, finds the place.*] Do you know what that Gallipoli campaign meant? Bugger all.

ALF [*lunging at him unsteadily*]. You——

[82]

HUGHIE. A face-saving device. An expensive shambles. [*Evading his father*] It was the biggest fiasco of the war. [*Starts to read rapidly.*] "The British were in desperate straits. Russia was demanding that the Dardanelles be forced by the British Navy and Constantinople taken. The Navy could not do it alone and wanted Army support." [*His father by now has stopped weaving groggily and stands watching him, trying to take it in.*] "Kitchener said the British Army had no men available." [*He looks up.*] So what did they do? The Admiralty *insisted* it be done no matter what the risk. Britain's Russian ally was expecting it. There was one solution. Australian and New Zealand troops had just got to Cairo for their initial training. Untrained men, untried. [*He looks quickly back at book.*] "Perhaps they could be used."

[*He snaps the book shut.* Perhaps. Perhaps they could be pushed in there, into a place everybody knew was impossible to take from the sea, to make the big gesture necessary . . . to save the face of the British. [*He turns on his father.*] . . . the British, Dad, the bloody Poms. THEY pushed those men up those cliffs, that April morning, knowing, KNOWING it was suicide.

WACKA [*roused*]. You don't know that. 'Ow could anyone know that?

HUGHIE. You know what it was like. [*Grabs the book open.*] Show them the maps. Show them the photos. A child of six could tell you men with guns on top of those cliffs could wipe out anyone trying to come up from below. And there were guns on top, weren't there, Wacka, weren't there?

ALF [*almost shocked sober*]. More credit to 'em, that's what I say, more credit to 'em they got up there and dug in.

HUGHIE. Oh yes, great credit to them—if you happen to see any credit in men wasting their lives.

ALF. Well, that's war, that's any war——

HUGHIE [*turning on him*]. Yes, and as long as men like you are fools enough to accept that, to say that, there'll always be wars.

ALF. You're tryin' to drag it down.

HUGHIE. It was doomed from the start, it was a waste! Every year you still march down that street with that stupid proud expression on your face you glorify the—bloody wastefulness of that day. [*He turns away quickly, sits panting and trembling.*]

ALF [*speechless for a moment, then, furious, he turns to the others*]. They don't care, do they? They don't believe in anything. What'd I tell you? What'd I tell you? The whole country's goin' down the drain. [*Then, turning on* HUGHIE] You telling him [*pointing to* WACKA] everything he's believed for forty years is wrong? You telling me what I've believed in is nothin'?

[*He makes a sudden dive at* HUGHIE, *drags him to his feet, but* HUGHIE *grabs him tightly and looks into his face.*

HUGHIE [*quiet and firm, less hysterical now*]. Believe in the men if you want to, they had guts. But the day . . . it's a mug's day.

ALF. Get away.

HUGHIE. Why remember it? Why go on and on remembering it? Oh yeah, "that's war, that's war" . . . Well, war's such a dirty thing I'd have thought as soon as it's over you'd want to forget it, be ashamed, as human beings, ashamed you ever had to take part in it.

ALF. Ashamed? Ashamed? To fight for your country?

HUGHIE. What did your country do for you after you'd fought? Arr . . . don't feed me all that.

MUM. Alf! [HUGHIE *breaks away from his father.*] [*To* HUGHIE] Was you thinkin' all that today when we watched him on the television? Was you thinkin' that and never said a word?

HUGHIE. I've been thinking it for years.

ALF [*turns to her*]. Did you see it? Did you see me in the march on that thing?

MUM. We did.

ALF [*to* HUGHIE]. There! You seen 'em. Decent blokes, decent lot of blokes marchin' with their mates. Two wars that represents, two wars you don't know nothin' about, you jumped-up little twerp. You can stand there and knock those men?

HUGHIE. Yes, I can. [*But he is faltering.*] They looked ridiculous.

ALF [*threateningly: a step closer to him*]. Yeah. Did they? How'd I look?

HUGHIE [*with sudden energy*]. I don't care how you looked then. It's how you look now. When you came in that door—when you came in that door—[*words, feelings tumble out of him*]—Oh, God, if you only knew how you looked. [*Pointing furiously at his mother and* WACKA] THEY laughed at you. [*To them*] How could you laugh? Why is a drunk man so funny? [*Then turning on his father*

[85]

again] Funny? Drunk or sober, you're not funny. You disgust me. You—*disgust*—*me*.

ALF. My kid! [*He flings himself at* HUGHIE. WACKA *gets hold of* ALF *and holds him back.* ALF *shouts and struggles.* HUGHIE *turns his back on them and strides to his bedroom, slamming the door.*]

MUM [*to* WACKA]. Get him out. I want to talk to Hughie.

WACKA. C'm'on, Alf. C'm'on. [*Struggling, swearing, shouting,* ALF *is dragged into kitchen where he collapses in chair, buries his head on table.*]

[*When they have gone* MUM *goes slowly, deliberately, to* HUGHIE'S *door, knocks on it.*

MUM [*sharply*]. Hughie! [*Silence.*] Hughie, listen to me. [*Silence.*] Hughie!

HUGHIE [*pressed against closet, shoulders heaving*]. What?

MUM. I want to know one thing. You going to publish that article?

HUGHIE. Leave me alone.

MUM. Because if you are and your father sees it, it's the finish, Hughie. You can pack your bags and leave. I mean it. [*He doesn't answer.*] Right?

HUGHIE [*defiantly*]. Right!

CURTAIN

[86]

ACT THREE

Early evening, some days later. ALF is in the kitchen cleaning his suit with white spirit. MUM is putting away last of dishes from evening meal, hangs up tea towel. Looks at him as though she wishes to say something. He avoids her eye.

She goes into lounge, switches on light. The TV set has gone. She does some half-hearted tidying up, stops near middle of room, stands aimlessly, thinking, restless. Then she goes to bookcase, takes out the encyclopaedia HUGHIE read from and sits in nearby chair. She is reading when ALF crosses through lounge on his way to their bedroom to hang up his suit. He glances at her without stopping, goes into bedroom. She turns a page. ALF comes back from bedroom. He seems about to return to kitchen but stands, hesitates, is unable to contain himself.

ALF. What d'yer lookin' at that thing for?

MUM [*not looking up*]. Ay?

ALF. What d'yer wanta read that thing for. Never looked at it in yr life before last week.

MUM. Free country.

      [ALF *seems about to burst into argument, restrains himself with a grunt and goes towards kitchen. Steps are heard outside. He turns. Looks towards front door.* HUGHIE *comes in. He has been hurrying, looks disturbed, unhappy. He and his father look at each other, look away.* HUGHIE *closes front door.* ALF *goes into kitchen.* HUGHIE *starts to go towards his bedroom, unzipping briefcase he carries.* MUM *has registered all this. As he moves she speaks.*] [*Quietly.*

MUM. Thought you was comin' home for tea.

HUGHIE. I had it up there.

MUM. What's the matter?

HUGHIE [*after hesitation*]. Nothing's the matter. [*But he doesn't move off.*]

MUM. All right. [*She returns to book.*]

HUGHIE. I had a row with Jan.

MUM. What about?

[*He hesitates then whips a newspaper out of his briefcase and holds it up for her to see.*

HUGHIE. Ah, nothing. This. [*Throws it on table.*]

[*She gets up, gapes at newspaper.*

MUM. You didn't . . .

HUGHIE. It's more than the story, we disagreed over the whole thing.

MUM [*still eyeing paper*]. Well? Go on.

HUGHIE [*about to speak, then*]. It's private.

MUM. Please y'self.

HUGHIE [*suddenly miserable*]. Mum—we agreed on everything, Jan and I, I thought we did.

UM [*comes towards him, with a shade more sympathy than usual*]. Is she worth worryin' about?

[88]

HUGHIE. Yes, she is. She's the first girl I ever met I really feel—— [*He stops.*]

MUM. Don't see it meself. [*He starts to go.*] Hughie . . . talk to your father.

HUGHIE. He won't talk to me.

MUM. I've had about enough, Hughie. Even when yr not here he gets round the house, won't hardly open his mouth. It's been days——

HUGHIE. I can't help it.

MUM. Yes, y'can. I'm sick of it, son.

> [ALF *comes in quickly, heading for bedroom.* HUGHIE *turns his back to him. With barely a glance towards* HUGHIE, ALF *speaks on the move.*]

ALF. I'm goin' up the pub, Mother.

MUM [*as he reaches bedroom door*]. Alf. [*He doesn't stop, goes into bedroom.*] [*She turns to* HUGHIE.] Hughie, please . . .

> [ALF *comes back, getting into old raincoat.*]

Alf . . . [*He strides towards door, she speaks more urgently*] Alf! [*He stops.*] Hughie. [*She is suddenly beginning to break, tries to toughen up*] Now, both of you, listen to me . . .

> [*They are both embarrassed.*]

I can't take much more. If you think it's any fun you two comin' and goin' never sayin' a word to each other . . . I can't stand much more.

ALF [*softly*]. Now, Dot.

MUM. Make it up. Both of you. Please. Make it up. For

[89]

my sake. [*She sits down abruptly, takes out handkerchief, blows her nose.*]

      [ALF *and* HUGHIE *look at each other, neither giving an inch.*

ALF. It's not my place. It's not my place to——

MUM. I don't care whose place it is. Someone has to go first.

ALF. It's not goin' t'be me.

      [HUGHIE *hasn't moved.*

MUM. I s'pose it's not goin' to be you neither. [*She looks from one to the other as they stare angrily across the room at each other*.] You couple of stiffnecked——

ALF. You get orf me back. [*He turns away, sits, his back ostentatiously to* HUGHIE. *A pause.* HUGHIE *walks down, stands behind his father.*]

HUGHIE [*a pause*]. I'm sorry. [*Quickly*] I'm sorry, Mum. [ALF *sits, head up, defiantly.*]

MUM [*to* ALF]. Go on. 'E's said 'e's sorry.

ALF [*without turning to* HUGHIE]. All right.

MUM. Alf.

ALF. 'Pology accepted.

HUGHIE. Thanks, Dad.

      [HUGHIE *goes towards his room*

MUM [*to* ALF, *sharply*]. That all?

ALF. Well, what d'y'want me to do? I accepted his apology.

MUM. Don't strain y'self.

HUGHIE. It's all right.

ALF. Hughie! [*Turns to address him directly, with attempt at dignity.*] Just one thing, my lad. I'll never agree with

what you had to say—you know what I'm referring to—
and I reckon you 'ad no right to say it in the same room
as me and Wacka after what we went through for you.
For you. Just don't mention it any more. That's my feelings. Understand?

HUGHIE. I wish I'd never said it either.

ALF [*expansively*]. Well! That's more like it. There y'are,
Mother, nothin' that a bit of friendly talkin' can't straigh-
ten out.

> [*He has moved up towards table.* HUGHIE *has spotted
> university paper lying where he dropped it and as his
> father nears it attempts to pick it up quickly.*

What's this? [ALF *picks it up, looks at front page.*] [*Excited*]
Mother! Look at this! Look at this! [*Beaming*] "See
Inside. Our Story on . . . Anzac Day." [*He fumbles
through pages to find it.*]

ALF. He done it. Fancy not tellin' us. There y'are, I knew
the silly little cow had his heart in the right place all the
time. After all that row he still put a wrap-up of the old
diggers in, after all. [*The paper is open.* MUM *watches
apprehensively.*] Listen to this. "Anzac Day, we are told
every year, is the day which comm—which commemorates
Australia's coming-of-age as a nation. One would never
know from the way it is . . ." [*He is suddenly doubtful*]
"observed". [*Looks up quickly at* MUM *then down at page
again.*] "Look at these frank pictures below. This is
the way Australia celebrates her national day . . ."

> [*He stares popeyed at the pictures. Then roars.*
Hughie!

> [HUGHIE *appears in the doorway.*

You——! You——! [*He is almost speechless.*] You take these pictures?

MUM. Alf, don't start again.

ALF [*almost shrieking*]. Look at 'em! Look at 'em! Men drunk—men fighting—look, a bloke vomitin'. YOU put that in there?

HUGHIE. You're not going to tell me it didn't happen.

ALF. Of course it happened, it always happens, you don't put that sorta thing in the paper——

HUGHIE. Why not?

ALF. You little hypocrite. A minute ago you was crawlin' to me, you was sorry y'd ever said——

HUGHIE. I didn't say I took it back. I don't take any of it back. I'm sorry because of the way I did it, to you and Wacka.

ALF [*looking at paper*]. Who wrote this? You write this? No, it was that girl.

HUGHIE. It was both of us.

ALF [*holds the paper out to* MUM]. Look at it, read it. Read it. [*Grabs it back from her.*] "It is a strange thing that men who for three hundred and sixty-four days have never given the nation a thought will on this day proclaim its greatness. How can it be great when—" [*His eyes bulge*] "—the winge-ers, whiners and no-hopers shoot their big mouths off on Anzac Day and do nothing the rest of the year round?" That little bitch! That——

MUM. Alf——

ALF. Shut up! Listen to it! LISTEN to it! "This is the day we are supposed to be proud. But . . ." [*He is sud-*

[92]

denly very quiet.] "I never feel more ashamed of being an Australian than I do on Anzac Day." [*A pause. He can't do anything but look at the paper and then stare at* HUGHIE.] Ashamed. Ashamed.

HUGHIE [*walking away from him*]. I'm not fighting with you over it, Dad.

ALF. You can't see past a few drunks. You can't. Is that all you saw the other day? Is it? [HUGHIE *won't answer.*] Is that all that day means to you? [HUGHIE *won't answer.*] Then I'm sorry for yer. I am. I'm sorry for yer. Well, what y'got to say to that? [HUGHIE *shakes his head. In disgust* ALF *turns to* MUM.] Are they all like that? All the kids today? They think like that?

HUGHIE. I don't care how the others think, that's how I think.

ALF. You'd take away everything. You'd take away the ordinary bloke's right to feel a bit proud of 'imself for once. You know what that march means? You saw it, on your television, you saw it. You know what that is? [HUGHIE *doesn't answer.*] March without uniforms, that's what that is. Y'don't get out there t'show what a great soldier y'was, y'r there as mates. Y'r there to say it was a job. Y'had to do it and y'done it. Together. Argue with that. Go on. Argue with that.

[HUGHIE *shakes his head.*

No, 'cause you can't. Every city, every little town in this country puts on its service and its march on that day. Every year for forty years they done it and they always will do it. Y'think this [*he shakes newspaper*] c'n make any

[93]

difference to it, a few pitchers and a few big words from a little squirt like you? Do yer?

[HUGHIE *doesn't answer.*

[*To* MUM] HE can't say anythin'. 'E can't say a word. [HUGHIE *has turned away, sits down. His father stands close, leans over him.*] Y'know why y'can't hurt it? Y'know why it's as strong as a rock? You ought to, cause you showed me. You said it yourself a week ago. And in that week I've seen it clearer than I ever did before. All them blokes like Wack 'n' me and the lot of 'em get out there for someth'n' there's not too many men in not too many countries in this world'd want to do. That's not a victory we're celebratin', son. It's a defeat. All right, you said it couldn't never be a victory. Well, it wasn't. They lost. But they tried. They tried, and they was beaten. A man's not too bad who'll stand up in the street and remember when 'e was licked. Ay?

HUGHIE [*quietly*]. Why not? Maybe it helps the great Australian laziness. Why worry about doing a good job? Fair enough's good enough. The only time we won our name was the time we lost.

ALF [*is momentarily taken aback at this jesuitical reasoning; covers quickly*]. That's real cunning, Hughie. Real cunning. [*Turns to* MUM] Y'know what I think? Y'c'n get too smart for y'r own good. That's what that boy's doin'. [*He hits his fingers against his own forehead.*] Everyth'n' comes from there. Nowhere else. Here. [*He turns to* HUGHIE.] Where's yr heart, Hughie? Hearts outa style with your new mob?

HUGHIE [*gets up quickly*]. I think I'd better go out.

[94]

MUM. Leave 'im alone, Alf, he's just had a row with his girl-friend.

ALF. Her? That little North Shore tart. That's where all 'is ideas are comin' from. She started it.

HUGHIE. No, Dad. You started it. You started it years ago when I was a kid. When you dragged me by the hand through mobs of them like this—[*gesturing towards newspaper*] just exactly like this. That's all I ever saw on Anzac Day, every year, year after year, a screaming tribe of great, stupid, drunken no-hopers.

ALF [*approaching him; very quietly*]. Hughie. I didn't hear that, did I? You didn't say that?

HUGHIE. I said it all right.

ALF [*evenly*]. Would you say it again?

HUGHIE. You've got to know, you'd better know once and for all how I feel. That's your famous old diggers to me. Great, stupid, drunken——

MUM. Alf!

> [*For he has back-handed his son viciously across the face.*
>
> [HUGHIE *staggers and is almost knocked off his feet. He collapses in chair, where he looks up at his father, astonished, but suddenly without anger.*

MUM. You get away from that boy.

ALF. That's men like my father he's talkin' about. Men who give their all.

MUM. Oh, give their all, where'd you read that? Don't talk rot.

ALF [*stunned*]. ROT?

MUM. Didn't cost yr old man much to go out in a blaze of glory. It's the ones like Wacka who come back knocked up and get nothin', just about nothin' and go on without a word the resta their lives, they're the ones who give their all.

ALF [*furiously, almost choking*]. Don't you turn on me now. I've had enough, Dot, don't you——

[*The front doorbell rings.*

MUM. Who the hell's that.

ALF. I don't want any visitors. Don't want any visitors tonight.

[MUM *has gone and opened door. It is* JAN.

JAN. Oh, Mrs. Cook, I'm sorry. I had to see Hughie.

[HUGHIE, *still nursing his face, gets up, startled.*

MUM. Come in. [JAN *comes in.* MUM *shuts door.* JAN *smiles nervously at* HUGHIE. MUM *comes back into room.*]

JAN. Mr. Cook, I had to see Hughie. You don't mind?

ALF. Mind? No, this is the new branch, the Uni's just opened a new wing 'ere. Make y'self at home. [*Then firmly.*] But I'd be obliged if y'd say what y've gotta say and get goin'. You've started enough trouble round here——

HUGHIE. Will you get it through your head Jan didn't start anything? The newspaper stunt was all my idea.

JAN. Oh, it's that.

ALF. I don't believe yer. Yr standin' up for 'er. Well, I stand up for what I believe too. And if that little jumped-up snob can put a story like that in a newspaper there's someth'n' the matter with this country.

JAN. Why? We all have to agree with you before we can get into print?

ALF. Don't you cheek me, young lady. I dunno what y'do in yr own home but yr not comin' here upsettin' things.

JAN. I'll upset who I like.

ALF. Don't you talk to me. I'm a bloody Australian——

JAN. You're so right, Mr. Cook. [*To* HUGHIE] Excuse me. I'm sorry I came. [*Starts to move away.*]

ALF. You hear 'er? You hear what she said to me? Nobody talks to me like that. I stood up and fought for this country. . . .

JAN [*turning quickly to face him*]. Mr. Cook——

HUGHIE. That'll do.

JAN. Mr. Cook. My father went to the war too—but he doesn't go on and on about it.

HUGHIE. OK, let it go——

JAN. You're nothing special, Mr. Cook. You're not the only hero on earth. You're just an ordinary little man.

ALF. Get her out! Get her out before I——

MUM. Leave her alone.

ALF [*beside himself with exasperation as they all gang up*]. I won't leave anyone alone, comes insultin' me and buggerin' up my son, who does she think she is, bringing her bloody upper-crust ways here. She talks about me, what did they ever do for Australia? Ay? What did they ever do?
    [JAN *faces back into room. Hesitates, then coolly.*

JAN. I just told you, Mr. Cook, but you never listen. They fought for it, as you did. They haven't done any more than you—but they haven't done any less either.
    [*It pulls him up short. He looks at each of them.*

[97]

ALF [to HUGHIE]. Get goin' with her. Go on. She wants t'talk t'yer. Get out in 'er car, talk about the great country it's gunna be when the whole mob's bright and clever like you. Go on. Get. Y'know where y'stand.

HUGHIE. Don't you push me around. Jan just tried to make you understand, you threw it back in her face. I'm sorry I stuck up for you now.

[*They are both startled by this slip.* ALF *is thrown a bit.*

ALF. When did you ever stick up for me?

HUGHIE. A while ago. Up there. We had a row about the whole thing. I took your part. Don't worry, it won't happen again.

[ALF *suddenly caves in, almost breaks down, he sits.* HUGHIE *looks closely at his father and drops his aggressiveness, clumsily.*

The paper just came out today. All the week I've been asking myself, why did I do it? After that night here—I didn't know what I was doing. One part of me said go ahead, print it, publish it. I wanted to all the more out of —sheer spite. But another part of me was fighting all the time. Saying to me: That isn't all the story, there is something more in Anzac still, even now, even if I can't see it. Then the deadline came up, I had to make up my mind. You weren't talking to me, home was pretty rotten to be in, I wanted to hit out. So . . . I did it. I went ahead with the story. I still don't know whether I should have or not.

[*A silence.*

[*It costs* ALF *a big effort to do so but at last he manages.*

[98]

ALF [*roughly*]. It's a free country. You got your opinion, you stick to it.

HUGHIE. But—— [*Hopelessly*] Oh, I don't know. Up there—at Uni—it seems terrific to be—outspoken and—critical and everything. But . . . [*He manages to face his father.*] I'm sorry. I didn't mean to hurt you.

ALF. Yes you did. Don't try to back out now. Go on. You go with her. She's right. [*Slowly he turns to face* JAN; *then quietly*] D'y' remember that job I was tellin' you about? [*With a half-smile*] The executive position?

JAN [*very quietly*]. Yes, Mr. Cook?

ALF. I didn't get it. Missed out. [*Quietly*] Too old. No qualifications. [*He turns to* HUGHIE *and* MUM.] I would've told you before—if we'd bin talkin'. You see? She's right.

[*He sits very stiffly, head up a bit, stiff-necked, and manages to say it without self-pity.*

I'm nothin'. I never bin anythin'. I know it. I was gunna be someth'n' when I was your age. I was. Well . . . now I drive a lift. [*A pause.*] It meant a lot to me, that new job. [*Looks up at* HUGHIE.] You don't think I haven't known for ages what you think of me? That job it would've been—my last chance to show my son I could—be someth'n'. . . .

HUGHIE. Dad . . .

ALF. I'm not the only one. Some of me old mates . . . when I think back to how we talked durin' the war . . . when I think back to what they wanted outa life. Some of 'em done all right. But even those in decent jobs—— [*Hesitantly, feeling it through*] It's more than jobs. It's . . . [*He stops. The others all watch him, reluctant to break in.*]

[99]

Boys I've known all me life. Went through the Depression with me, then the War. They're nothin' much either. Nothin' much . . . [*Beneath his control he is trembling.*] But for one day they're someth'n'. [*Quietly*] Anzac Day. They make a fuss of y' for once. The speeches and the march . . . and y're all mates. Y're mates an' everyth'n' seems all right. The whole year round I look forward to it. Me mates, some grogs, and—and the feelin' y're not just . . . not just . . . [*He shakes his head.*] Y'know. [*He gets up, seems about to go, but turns to them.*] It's the one day . . . the one day . . . [*He is almost unable to speak.*] I ever feel . . .

> [*They all look at him in profound embarrassment. He turns and goes quietly to kitchen.*

MUM [*uncomfortably*]. Poor old bugger. [*To* JAN] He knows 'e ain't up to much, why'd y'ave to rub it in?

JAN. Mrs. Cook. [*Goes to her.*] I'm sorry, honestly I am——

MUM [*patting her hand without thinking*]. Never mind, love, it's not your fault. That Hughie started it.

HUGHIE [*with a kind of wonder*]. I was sorry before. But I'm not now. I don't know why but I'm not. [*Very close to his mother*] Gee, I love him, Mum.

MUM [*not cracking*]. Yeah. All right.

> [*She goes to kitchen.* HUGHIE *and* JAN *face each other uncomfortably. He goes to table, gets cigarettes.*

HUGHIE. Cigarette?

> [*She nods. He gives her one and lights up for her.*

JAN. Do you want me to go?

HUGHIE. What's the use? The whole thing was so easy for you.

JAN. Hughie, I know that. You *had* to make your statement—as a man. Force them to accept it. I'm glad you did, still glad.

HUGHIE. A man? [*Quietly*] I feel as though I've been a priggish, hysterical kid, shooting his mouth off at something he's never understood. I *thought* I understood, I'd read all the books. The books don't tell you enough. [*He is struggling to make it clear to himself.*] It's funny . . . I still dislike it as much as I ever did. But I know what they *feel* about it now.

JAN. Oh, don't be so damned sentimental. Nothing's changed just because one old man got upset. Anzac Day's still the same ghastly thing it always was.

HUGHIE [*exploding*]. Who CARES about Anzac Day? I've got all that off my chest. [*Excited at his self-discovery.*] You see, it wasn't just that, it never was.

JAN. I know. It was him.

HUGHIE. It was him. I was hitting out at him. Everything about him. He's yesterday, he's the past. They both are. So they are. So I've got to put up with it. [*Suddenly almost breaking*] Avea cuppa tea, luv, go on, avea cuppa tea. I don't want, I don't want, I don't WANT a cuppa tea. [*He collapses into a chair.*] Jan, I hate it here. Hate it.

JAN [*rushing to him*]. Then don't stay. Leave. Break free. You'll have to sooner or later. They're wonderful people, Hughie, I should never have spoken as I did, but—you'll never grow up properly until you can stand on your own feet without them.

HUGHIE. Maybe. Maybe I'll never grow up until I can learn to accept them as they are. And not be ashamed of them.

JAN. Ashamed? Hughie.

HUGHIE. My father thought you were a snob. *I'm* the snob. I can't help it. Jan, I can't BREATHE in this house. Everything they say and do just jars and jars on me. They're so—they're—I don't know—they're so— oh, I can never find the word. It's just that they're so . . . [*a long moment as the word comes to him at last*] they're so—Australian.

JAN. Are they? They're what it was. We're what it's going to be. [*Smiles.*] You're going to stay, aren't you.

HUGHIE [*nods*]. I'll walk out that door one day, Jan, I know I will. But not now. When I saw him sitting there, I made a pact with myself. I won't walk out on him now. You saw what losing that job's done to him. I don't care how rugged it gets here. For the time being I'll stay.

JAN. And I'm no use any more? [*He doesn't answer.*] But I'll help you. Help you.

HUGHIE. All right, you'll help me. And patronise my family without meaning to. And fight with your mother all the time—until you get sick of the whole thing and drift back to the Yacht Club.

JAN [*hurt*]. Hughie.

HUGHIE. You'll be able to laugh and tell them about your proletariat phase . . .

JAN [*quietly, stubbing out cigarette*]. As nice and polite a—brushoff as I ever heard. Well . . . so long, Hughie Cook. [*She moves towards door.*] See you around.

HUGHIE. I don't know that you will. I think I might ditch my course. Leave Uni.

JAN [*coming back*]. You can't do that. Hughie, you mustn't.

HUGHIE. That damned University's taking me farther away from them every minute.

JAN. I see. You do all the giving-in. To your father. Why shouldn't he give a bit too?

HUGHIE. He'll meet me halfway. After tonight it'll be better. He'll meet me halfway. And even if he can't . . . [*He smiles.*] I made a pact with myself. Goodbye, Jan.

JAN. Hughie. You've got to believe one thing. Please. About you and me. I wasn't just——

HUGHIE. Slumming?

JAN. Hughie, don't. Can't you——? Can't you see I——?
[*She can't manage to say it and hurries blindly to door, opens it, takes one last look back at him, then composes herself and walks out slowly with an attempt at self-possession and pride.*
[*He stands staring after her, then moves quickly after her. But as he reaches door he restrains himself, comes slowly back, sees cigarette in ashtray, slowly stubs it out. Then, bracing himself, he goes steadily towards the kitchen.*

[ALF *sits at table, beer in front of him, head down.* MUM *is at sink making tea.* HUGHIE *goes to her, with forced brightness.*

HUGHIE. Going out tonight, Mum?

MUM. Haven't thought about it. Don't think so.

HUGHIE. Why don't we all go to the local flicks? There's a musical on—a good one, I mean, not just rock-'n'-roll. It got good writeups . . . You like a good musical, don't you? Why don't we all go and have a look at it?

MUM [*a doubtful glance at* ALF]. See how we all feel later on. [*Very gently*] Wanta cuppa tea?

[*He shakes his head.*

[WACKA *appears at back door of kitchen.*

WACKA. G'day all. How y' goin'?

ALF [*roughly*]. Come in and siddown.

[WACKA *sits.* ALF *pours beer for him.*

WACKA. 'Ow are y', 'Ughie?

ALF [*quietly*]. We had a fight. [WACKA *looks from father to son.*] I hit him. That's what it's come to. I hit my son.

WACKA [*a pause*]. I bin waitin' for that.

ALF. All right. You know everything. [*To the room at large*] He knows everything. He'd stand there and be insulted. You stood there and let him insult you. Well, not me. Not me.

MUM. Where'd it get you?

ALF. Well, now I know. I know what my son and his mob think of me. Well, all right, if he prefers to get around with that lot—— [*He has still not looked at* HUGHIE.]

[104]

HUGHIE. I'm here, aren't I?

ALF [*turns to him; quietly*]. Yeah? For how long?
  [*A break.* HUGHIE *is having one of his small battles
  with himself. Finally he turns to them.*

HUGHIE. Dad. Mum . . . I want to talk to you about something. Dad . . . [*He moves towards table.*] I think I might
leave Uni.

MUM. What for?

ALF [*gaping at him*]. Leave——? Leave University? What
the hell do you want to do that for?

HUGHIE. I thought you knew what for. I'm sick of
feeling—mixed up. You know it's changed me, I can
tell how you both feel. Well—I want to do the right
thing.

ALF. And what sort of work d'y' think y'd do?

HUGHIE. Drive a truck, take photos, anything.

ALF [*on his feet*]. Oh no you don't. Oh no you don't!! You
think I spent my whole life trying to get you somewhere
to have you throw it away now? What's the matter
with you? Don't you want to better y'self? Y'r gettin'
chances blokes like me and Wacka in our young days
we'd've given anything to have. And you're not satisfied.

HUGHIE. I'm never SURE of myself. Wherever I am,
whoever I'm with, I feel—I just feel—I'm forever uncomfortable.

ALF. Well, who said life was s'posed to be comfortable?
Where'd y'ever get the idea it was anythin' but a bloody
battle all the way? Battle! That's what it is. Just like
fightin' in a war. You dunno whether you're gunna win or

lose and in the long run it don't much matter, it's the fightin' that's important. Some people fight all their lives for someth'n' and never win, never win, end up with bugger-all. But at least they had a go. You'd give it away as easy as that. Gawd. What's the country coming to?

HUGHIE [*exasperated*]. I was thinking of you. God, I don't know, whatever you do round here's wrong.

[ALF *has suddenly grabbed him by the shirtfront and in a final complete fury is shaking the boy.*

ALF. I felt like knocking your block off in there and I still might, I still might. You're gunna stay at that University till y've done the lot. And if it's a battle for you, right, it's a battle.

[*He releases him, sits abruptly, pours a beer.*
[HUGHIE *turns to his mother.*

MUM. He's right.

[*A moment as* HUGHIE *thinks of his future.*

HUGHIE [*firmly*]. But you won't like it. Because I can't— just to make you happy—I can't change how I think and feel. About—the most important things. [*He turns to* WACKA.] Wacka, I haven't apologised to you for last week. I'm sorry if I offended you or hurt you. But—— [*to his father*] I'm not sorry I said or did those things. I still believe them. I'd do them again.

MUM [*looks from* ALF *to* HUGHIE]. I dunno who's worst.

HUGHIE [*to* ALF]. I want us both to know how we stand. [ALF *nods, but won't look at him*] I *don't* respect what you all do on that day. I never will. And I don't respect what

[106]

it stands for. But now I respect the way you feel about it, and if I'm going to stay here . . . [ALF *looks up at him quickly*] that'll have to be enough. Now—do you still want me?

ALF [*battling*]. I want you to have an education. I do. I do. But—— [*Suddenly unable to cope with it any more bursts out to* WACKA] He goes too far, he gets above himself. They're all the same now, they think they run the country. Kids! Kids! You scrimp and save and give'm everything. For what? For what?

WACKA. Alf. [*It is quiet enough but they all turn to him. He hesitates, self-conscious as ever, then gently*] Your boy's growing up. You've got to face that. He's got the right to think and say what he likes. Any fightin' we ever did, you'n' me, in any wars, it was to give him that right. And if we don't agree with what he thinks—[*stops, then*] —well, it's his world. We've had it. He's got it all ahead of him.

[*He turns to* HUGHIE. *A little shy smile.*

Only—give the old blokes a bit of a go sometimes, son.

[*He looks down at table.* ALF *pushes a glass towards* WACKA, *ignores* HUGHIE. MUM *looks to her son to see what he will do.*

[HUGHIE *has listened intently and with sudden respect to* WACKA, *and now, managing a smile, he comes slowly towards his father. But as his father begins to speak, the smile vanishes.*

ALF. That's all right about him. That's all right. I'm a bloody Australian and I'll always stand up for bloody Australia. I seen these jumped-up cows come and go,

[107]

come and go, they don't mean a bloody thing, what did they ever do for the country, they never did nothing. It's the little man, he's the one goes out and gets slaughtered, we're the ones they get when the time comes, we're the ones, mugs, the lot of us, mugs. He said that. He said it. Did my son say that? Did he say that about me and my mates? That's good men he's talking about, men who give their all, that's decent men. I'll show the little cow. Someone's gotta show these kids. I'll show him, I know what he thinks, I'm nothin', but I'll show him, I'll show the lot of 'em. I'm a bloody Australian and I'll always . . .

[*Through this* MUM *has stood very still, watching* ALF. *Then her gaze has gone to* HUGHIE *as he backs away slowly, hurt and disappointed. When he reaches the kitchen door he turns and hurries blindly into the main room.*

[ALF *has continued nonstop but as he reaches his last words he falters and stops as though really hearing his own voice for the first time. Slowly he pushes the beer away, looks off after* HUGHIE, *head raised a little, almost waiting to hear a door slam.*

[*Alone in the other room* HUGHIE *stands, angry and bewildered, and then charges towards the front door. He flings it open, but as he is about to dash out something holds him. He stands trembling, battling, and then slams the door. Head back,* ALF *listens, listens. Slowly* HUGHIE *comes back into lounge and sits down.*

CURTAIN